"Wh-what are you licking her lips

Ryan unbuttoned his shorts and dropped them to the floor.

"Oh, my God," she whispered, reaching up to clutch her throat.

"Nothing you haven't seen before, is it, Jade? Though you didn't stick around long enough to really see how you affected me last night."

She could see it now, though. Her whole face was flushed as she stared at him. All of him, including the erection he wasn't trying to hide.

He'd always assumed he was a normally built man. But the shocked hunger in her eyes told him he'd caught her off guard.

"No, you're right. I d-didn't see you that well," she stammered.

He just stood in front of her, completely naked. Uncaring, not bothering even to pretend to be self-conscious.

She looked as if she wanted to run. She looked as if she wanted to jump on him. She looked as if she needed someone to tell her what to do.

So he did.

"Take off your dress and get into the bed, Jade."

Dear Reader,

I just love Southern cities. Though I was born in Virginia, I wasn't really raised in the South. But I have always been intrigued by the rich culture, passion and romance of the region. One city in particular, Savannah, has always fascinated me. So when I decided to write a book about a sultry possible-thief, I couldn't think of any better city to put her in than Savannah.

Jade's not like a lot of my heroines. She's more self-confident, and a lot more mysterious. But I really liked exploring her quirky love of history, her legacy and ancestry, not to mention her wicked sense of revenge, which would allow her to tie a naked man to a statue...and leave him there.

Hmm...enter naked man. Ryan Stoddard. Northern, conservative, professional. But since he also has vengeance on his mind, he's more than up to the challenge of tackling Jade head-on. Handcuffs and all.

Hope you enjoy my atmospheric little visit to this lovely Southern city. I enjoyed it so much I think I'll return there in the future. In person. And in my books.

Best wishes,

Leslie Kelly

Books by Leslie Kelly

HARLEQUIN TEMPTATION
882—TWO TO TANGLE
916—WICKED & WILLING
948—TRICK ME, TREAT ME

HARLEQUIN BLAZE
62—NATURALLY NAUGHTY

LESLIE KELLY
Wickedly Hot

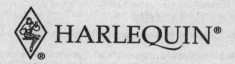

HARLEQUIN®

TORONTO • NEW YORK • LONDON
AMSTERDAM • PARIS • SYDNEY • HAMBURG
STOCKHOLM • ATHENS • TOKYO • MILAN • MADRID
PRAGUE • WARSAW • BUDAPEST • AUCKLAND

To Karen and Lynn...thanks for helping me plot this one while we floated in my pool last summer.

And to all the wonderful reviewers and Webmistresses who help support this genre, particularly Barb Hoeter, Barb Hicks, Carla Hosom, Blythe Barnhill, Kathy Boswell, Catherine Witmer, Cynthia Penn and Diana Tidlund. We couldn't do this job without your support and enthusiasm.

RECYCLED PAPER · RECYCLED PAPER

ISBN 0-373-69191-2

WICKEDLY HOT

Prologue

LYNNETTE GRAYSON HAD finally found the perfect woman for her grandson Ryan and she was utterly determined to bring them together. Whether he liked it or not.

"Brunette, his favorite," she murmured as she went over her checklist. "Intelligent, without question. Tall and slim, somewhat mysterious." And, most of all, *interesting*.

Ryan was altogether too comfortable, too spoiled, too at ease in his Manhattan apartment with his equally bored friends. He lived for his job with a high-stakes architecture firm, dated far too many women and cared for none of them.

He needed someone to challenge him. "Someone to spice him up a bit," Lynnette said, remembering the horridly cold creature Ryan had brought to dinner the last time his grandparents had come into the city.

Her grandson wasn't cold. That big, cold city might have made him forget he came from exciting, passionate, fascinating people who loved quickly and loved forever. Herself included, she had to admit with a smile. She'd led her husband, Edward, on a merry chase before marrying him, but she'd known he was the one from the first time he'd held her hand.

"Women nowadays," she said aloud with a disgusted sigh. "No mystery. No subtlety. No uniqueness."

Except for *her*. Jade Maguire, the young woman from Savannah she'd met just last week.

Jade was exactly what Ryan needed. The perfect woman at the perfect moment. Ryan was thirty years old. It was high time for him to settle down, create a family. Her other grandchildren were all happily settled, having followed family tradition by falling madly in love with the right person as soon as they'd met them. She wouldn't rest until the same thing happened to Ryan—the oldest and, though she'd never admit it aloud, her favorite.

Unfortunately, she had the feeling he would be a little stubborn about this.

She'd tried matchmaking before with, er, *unfortunate* results. This wasn't the same. She wasn't inviting him up for a weekend when she'd coincidentally invited a young woman she'd met at the bank. Nor was it like the time she'd hosted a dinner party, with Ryan and the granddaughter of a friend the only unattached people there. This wasn't like the florist, or the schoolteacher, or that nice young girl who sold houses for a living. None of whom Ryan had found the least bit interesting, much less fallen madly in love with in record time.

No, this time she'd chosen wisely. Perfectly, as a matter of fact. An art lover, a historian, a fascinating young woman who'd built a business all on her own. Even her business was exciting, unique and mysterious, like its owner.

Jade Maguire ran one of those wonderfully spooky walking tour companies in the old Southern city of Savannah. Lynnette had never taken such a tour, but the adventurous part of her told her she'd probably love being scared out of her wits while standing on a darkened street late at night. Jade had told them a few fascinating, ghostly tales when she'd come to see Lynnette about the painting that used to hang above the fireplace.

"Imagine," Lynnette murmured aloud, looking at the now-empty wall where the beautiful portrait of a young woman had hung. "We had stolen property."

Lynnette's great-great-grandfather had stolen the portrait from a plantation during the Civil War. Jade had produced positive proof—letters, a copy of a social column from an ancient newspaper, even a copy of the wrinkled, yellowed, hand-written bill of sale from the artist.

Jade had asked Lynnette and her husband to consider donating the painting to the Savannah Historical Society, either now or in the future. Lynnette had immediately agreed, not only because it was the right thing to do but also because she was already trying to figure out a way to get her grandson Ryan to go visit the painting in Savannah.

Not likely. He'd certainly never do it because she asked him to. He'd know something was up and would suspect a romantic fix-up.

So she had to be careful. Tricky. Never ever let Ryan know she was trying to bring him together with Jade Maguire.

"How?" she whispered, still staring at the empty place on the wall. And suddenly, as with most of her *really* good ideas, it simply popped into her head

She was smiling as she reached for the phone. Smiling as she dialed and listened to the ring. But when Ryan answered, she quickly mustered up a quivery, weak, old-lady voice and some tears. He wouldn't be taken in by much. Her grandson had always, however, had a soft spot for a woman who cried.

"Ryan?"

"Grandmother, what's wrong?"

"I need you," she said. "You see, I'm afraid I've been swindled." Crossing her fingers behind her back and sending up a promise to say an extra Act of Contrition the next time she went to mass, she proceeded directly to the biggest whopper of her life. "A dreadful con woman has stolen the painting my father left me."

1

JADE MAGUIRE CIRCLED the ballroom of the historic old Medford House Inn and Museum, socializing with the Savannah elite, but never taking her eyes from her prey. He stood out, impossible to miss amongst the ladies in glittering gowns and the men in their pressed tuxedos. Though he'd made the concession of allowing the customary gardenia bloom to be tucked into his lapel, he no more resembled the spoiled, wealthy pillars of Southern society than Jade resembled a Barbie doll.

Though his elegant suit fit his tall, hard form with tailored precision, it was a dark navy instead of the *de rigueur* black. That only drew more attention to his already striking looks. His shoulders and chest were too brawny to be considered tasteful. His dark hair too long over his brow for most men of high standing. His eyes—which from a distance appeared light, a nice contrast against his hair—moved constantly over the crowd. Searching, hunting, seeking, though she didn't know what.

His body shifted with an almost-disguised impatience that hinted at boredom. But every once in a while his gaze found her. And lingered. She always looked away, aware of the full force of his attention from across the crowded room. It was accompanied by masculine appreciation, which was good considering her plan.

But it also unnerved her. It dug at her, prying into her life, silently looking for answers to unvoiced questions. Hinting that he wasn't just a simple mark, an easy quarry for her scheme.

All in all, he was much too attractive for a miserable, loathsome creep.

"Ryan Stoddard," she whispered, tasting the hated name on her lips for the dozenth time today.

"Have you met him?"

She immediately turned her attention to Tally Jackson, local matriarch and Jade's godmother. Jade didn't have to ask who she meant. Every woman here tonight had been giving the tall, dark stranger second looks. And third ones. "No."

Tally flapped her fan, which matched her old-fashioned, hoop-skirted evening gown. She'd chosen to come in full costume, not mere formal wear, since she was representing the historical society at tonight's gala. "But you want to."

"Not particularly."

The older woman gave a sound of disbelief too elegant to be called a snort, but not far from it. "Well, he certainly appears to want to meet you." When Jade shrugged, Tally added, "Or just to *want* you."

"Maybe he's going to get his wish," Jade murmured. "But only when it comes to *meeting* me."

Tally smirked, obviously thinking the man could get around any woman's defenses. Including Jade's, which had been in place for quite some time now. "If you say so."

Tally was a distant cousin—like many others in Savannah—and seemed to think she knew Jade as well as she knew herself. Maybe that was true. The older woman had, after all, helped shape the woman Jade had become. A fixture in her life since childhood, Tally had long cultivated Jade's love for local history. Along with Jade's mama, and great-aunt Lula Mae, Tally had told her endless stories that had enthralled and captivated her as a little girl. The three women had instilled in Jade a sense of belonging, of home, of pride, until Jade had come to understand that Savannah's history was inextricably wound with her own.

This place defined her.

From her earliest childhood memories, Jade had felt the presence of generations of Dupré women who'd preceded her. She'd seen herself in every role—matriarch to mistress, slave to debutante. Like Savannah, the Dupré women were dark but graceful, sometimes ruthless but always elegant. Genteel but often boiling with emotion and passion.

When they loved, they loved hard, and usually only once. When they lost, they grieved but moved on. They seemed destined to never fill an emptiness inside that longed for a certain something out of reach—whether it was a way of life, or a loved one—but they found a way to live with it.

Jade had learned *that* lesson at a young age, too, when her father had died.

"Now, aren't you glad you came?" Tally asked. "If only to see that lovely man? I don't believe I've seen that look in your eye in a good year, young lady."

"You're imagining things." Then, because she didn't want to offend Tally, she added, "But yes, I'm glad I came."

Tally was the one who'd talked Jade into coming to this party tonight. Thank heaven she had, given Stoddard's presence. Normally Jade avoided such functions. But since she'd just helped arrange for the return of a long-lost sapphire necklace—which had been stolen from this plantation home during the Civil War—Jade had allowed Tally to persuade her.

"I wish you'd let me introduce you and reveal your help in getting the necklace donated."

Jade immediately shook her head. "Not part of the deal. I don't need recognition. You know that's not why I do this. Mama likes the spotlight, I don't."

Her work provided satisfaction enough. Researching and tracking down historical items and persuading their present-day owners to return them to their rightful places—well, it was merely a hobby, but it fascinated her. Just as she was fascinated by these stately homes with their seething pasts.

Besides, seeing that necklace so proudly displayed here in the small museum was all the payoff she needed.

Tally harrumphed, knowing she'd lose the argument again. Then she glanced at Ryan Stoddard. "Shall I slip him your phone number so you can pretend you're not making the first move?"

Jade tore her attention off the necklace—on loan here tonight before being moved to a larger local museum run by Tally's society—and frowned at her overly romantic godmother. "Absolutely not. I can arrange my own introduction, thank you."

"You need more than an introduction," Tally said in disgust. "Darlin', you need a shove into a naked man's arms."

Jade raised a brow. "I somehow don't think I'm going to land in a naked man's arms immediately after an introduction."

Something like that might happen to Jenny, the flighty member of their family. But not Jade. Not the mysterious one.

Tally smiled, catlike. "Well, now, that depends on who does the introducin'."

Tally had been looking for a love life for Jade for two years, ever since Jade had ended a relationship with a man she'd cared about but who'd never really understood her. He'd asked one too many times, *Who wants to make a living telling ghost stories?* Rick had never appreciated or respected the kind of life she'd chosen for herself.

Respect was important to Jade. Having come from a family who'd done without it a lot of the time, she was determined never to feel lower than anyone else. Any man in her life had to be one she respected in return. One who could match her in wits, challenge her in ideas, and keep her on her toes. He had to support her choices, no matter how crazy her life got. With her family, her life sometimes got *really* crazy.

And she had to love him beyond all reason.

So far, she hadn't met such a man. She certainly wouldn't here, tonight, with all the rich snobs looking down their noses at her—a member of *that* side of the famous local family.

"You never know what can happen at a first meeting," Tally said, apparently not noticing Jade's distraction.

"Actually I do," Jade said. "Remember the handsome guy who came on the garden walking tour a few years ago, saying he was looking for movie locations?"

"The producer?"

"He wasn't."

"He whisked you off to his fabulous place on the beach."

Jade crossed her arms. "Not his."

Tally sounded a little less enthusiastic as she asked hopefully, "He drove that beautiful sports car?"

"Rented."

"Well, darling, I hear *this* man," she nodded toward the dark-haired, blue-suited stranger, "is exactly who he claims to be. A nationally known, wealthy, professional architect. So if at first you didn't succeed...try again."

"No." Jade ignored the older woman's hopeful look. "And don't say a word to my mother about this. It's not what you think." She lifted her drink to her lips, murmuring, "It's a private matter. One I need to clear up with him."

"A matter of getting naked and between the sheets?"

Rolling her eyes, she ignored Tally's salacious chuckle. "No. Now go mingle. Be sociable. Rule the world through your glove-covered iron fist. I think I see someone wearing cream-colored shoes with a taupe dress. Go skewer her with that sharp tongue of yours."

Tally gave a delicate shiver. "Hideous. Money truly is wasted on the color-blind and those one generation out of the trailer park."

Jade chuckled, knowing Tally herself was only *two* generations out of the trailer park.

The older woman's eyes lit up, spying a wealthy older man who'd recently moved to town. Jade recognized the look. Tally was a fund-raiser supreme.

"Right on time," Tally whispered, greeting the man with a languid little wave of her hand. "That's Leonard something-or-other from Chicago. He's here with his wife who wears altogether too much jewelry. I have to make nice with them before somebody tells her only tarts and carpetbaggers' wives wear so much jewelry to an event like this."

"Nobody here would say it—except you. Now be nice or I'll warn your prey to hide his wallet."

That reminded Jade of her own victim. She began to look around for Ryan Stoddard, target of her search-and-destroy mission. Searching hadn't been tough—he'd certainly stood out. The destroying part might be more difficult. But he deserved it.

Anyone who broke the heart of her baby sister deserved destroying. He was just lucky Jade was only going to humiliate him, not castrate him like she'd prefer to do.

"There is one other person who could get away with saying such a thing," Tally said, after probably trying to decide whether or not Jade had been paying her a compliment. "Your mama. I wish she hadn't chosen this month to go on her cruise. I need her here."

"It *is* her honeymoon," Jade said, not bothering to keep a dry note from her voice.

"What's one more honeymoon to your mama?"

That sentence, in a nutshell, could probably explain Jade's entire life. They'd each had their own ways of dealing with Daddy's death more than a dozen years ago. Jade had grown mature before her time. Jenny had settled firmly into her role of spoiled baby. And Mama had just kept getting married, hoping she'd find someone else to love as much as she'd loved Daddy.

A shrink would probably say their past explained why Jade felt so protective of her sister, Jenny. It had been the two of them, facing the zaniness of their world with a much-married mother and a scandalous family, for a long time. Though only five years older, Jade had become so used to mothering her sister that she sometimes forgot they were just siblings.

It incensed Jade to remember the tears on her sister's cheeks. Jenny deserved some payback for what Ryan Stoddard had done to her. And Jade was going to see that she got it.

"Jade? Are you listening to me?"

She returned her attention to Tally. "Of course. But I have to say, this time I think Mama's finally met her match. A man with money who doesn't let her tell him what to do."

Tally nodded. "I have high hopes, too. But I do miss her. I needed her tonight. I don't suppose you..."

Jade narrowed her eyes and shook her head. "Don't even think about it. I'm not one of your society matrons. Most people in this room have no idea who I am, and I like it that way."

Tally frowned. The argument was an old one.

"Besides," Jade added, "if I want somebody to drop dead, I'll tell them to drop dead. Not, 'How delightful you look, sugah. Oh, I just love your hair. Why, it's almost exactly the shade and style of my grandma's French poodle.'"

Tally chuckled as Jade laid on a heavy Southern accent, which was nearly nonexistent in her everyday speech. "You're rather good at that."

"I don't want to be," Jade replied.

And she didn't. No matter how much her mother and her cohorts had tried to teach her, Jade had never learned to *enjoy* being sweet while cutting, honest while evasive. She much preferred direct insults to veiled ones, outright lies to such intricate games.

Though, tonight she was setting herself up for a very intricate one, wasn't she? The thought made her return her attention to the dark-haired stranger. She shivered a little. *Intricate games, indeed.*

"'Bye, darling, have fun," Tally said. Then she greeted the rich northerner with an air kiss and a gushing compliment on his clip-on tie, which Jade knew must be driving Tally mad.

Jade watched, then whispered, "Time to move."

As she sipped her drink—ginger ale with a twist of lime, which would appear to most to be alcoholic—she scanned the crowd again. Even if she hadn't been looking for the man when she'd shown up here tonight, she knew her eyes would have sought him out anyway. Just as any woman looked at something she desired but couldn't have.

Only, Jade meant to *have* him.

Earlier, his blue suit had stood out in the sea of black tuxes and brightly colored gowns, but she didn't spot him at first. Then finally she found him, leaning indolently against an arched doorway leading to another room.

Watching her.

He'd been watching *her.*

She flushed slightly. *Darn. Caught off guard.*

The man's eyes met hers from across the room. Blue. Or green. Surrounded by lush lashes and topped by dark brows that were slightly raised as he caught her stare.

Then he smiled.

Her legs wobbled. Good lord, no man had made her legs wobble since she was twelve and her Cajun second cousin had visited from New Orleans. Stoddard was altogether too big. Too ruggedly handsome. Too powerful-looking to play games with.

Yet that's exactly what Jade planned to do. Play games with him. And then leave him in the dirt.

But why is he here?

She didn't mean why was he here in Savannah. She knew why—for a big architects' convention, conveniently scheduled in her home city this year. The convention had saved her from traveling to New York to track him down.

But she'd expected him to stay at the hotel adjoining the convention center. Finding out from a friend at the hotel that he wasn't registered there had been a shock. Even more of a shock had been learning he was staying here at the Medford House.

Ryan Stoddard had no business being in this secluded, exclusive little piece of Savannah society. No business at all. He should be sitting in a loud hotel bar with the sounds of tinkling glasses and businessmen comparing last year's sales figures. Scoping out the women, flirting while they wondered how far they could go without technically cheating on their wives.

Not here, amid the husky laughter of bored millionaires and the scent of jasmine and magnolia that permeated the room from open French doors leading out to the lush grounds. Not in this place which many decades ago would have held tobacco planters and wounded veterans, as opposed to the bankers and stock brokers who comprised the elite set these days.

This was *her* turf. And damned if she wanted him on it. She'd planned to launch her attack on his ground, then slip away, back into the shadows of hers, where he'd never find her.

No way could she implement her original plan. A big chain hotel would have been simple—a pickup in a bar, a trip to his room, a heated encounter. Then walking out, laughter on her lips, leaving him naked and humiliated as he realized he'd been had. Realized he wasn't going to get off scot-free for breaking the heart of a member of her family.

"Jenny," she whispered, still missing her only sibling.

Her sister had gone off to try to be a star on the stage in New York City, against the family's wishes and to

Mama's utmost horror. She'd landed on the stage, all right—a raised platform in a diner where she served chicken noodle soup and pastrami on rye between showstopping numbers.

She'd seemed happy enough, though, at least until last week when she'd come home for Mama's wedding. Jenny had been crying about a man she'd met at the restaurant. She'd fallen *hard* as only a vulnerable, lonely twenty-one-year-old could. The stranger had swept her off her feet then dropped her flat.

Ryan Stoddard, aka the bastard.

It was time for him to pay. If Aunt Lula Mae found out, she'd likely want to punish him herself. And it still might come to that. If Jade couldn't publicly humiliate him, she just might have to get some of his hair and let Lula Mae do what she did best—curse him so he'd never be able to, uh, *perform* again.

But not until she'd given it a shot. Her way.

Which meant Ryan Stoddard was in for the most embarrassing night of his life.

RYAN HADN'T EXPECTED her to be so beautiful.

She stood out like an exotic jungle flower among a bunch of daisies. Her silky-looking dark hair was nearly black, skimming over her shoulders and down her back until it was lost against the color of her dress. A soft, red scarf draped loosely across her shoulders provided a dramatic contrast that drew the eye again and again.

Her skin was smooth and perfect, a warm tanned color like fine coffee full of rich, sweet cream. She was taller than most of the men who'd been eyeing her all evening, and held her slender jaw slightly up, indicating confidence and perhaps a bit of arrogance.

Though in a crowd, she seemed alone. Her detached attitude was enticing because of its mysterious quality, but off-putting because of her disinterest in her surroundings.

Her body was sin, her face was flawless, her eyes were wicked.

How appropriate for a thief.

"Mr. Stoddard, are you enjoying yourself?"

Mamie Brandywine, the owner of the bed-and-breakfast and museum, joined him. She briefly pulled his attention off his target, the woman he'd come to Savannah to find. Jade Maguire.

"Very nice, thank you."

"And you're finding your tours of the local plantation homes helpful in your research?"

"Absolutely," he said, trying to get his mind off the seductive, deceitful temptress and back on his job. Something he'd been putting on the back burner for the past few weeks while trying to get retribution for what had been done to his grandmother. Fortunately, his quest for justice had led him here, to the very city he needed to visit while writing an article on the architecture of the Old South.

"I'm truly enjoying the tours you've set up. Thanks so much for arranging for me to stay in some of the local inns," he added, trying to find some basic element of charm—or at least cordiality—within himself. It had been buried beneath a layer of anger for weeks.

That anger had increased the moment he'd seen Jade Maguire. She should have looked like a thief, a crone, a crook.

But she didn't. She looked like every man's fantasy. The kind of woman he'd always imagined but never found—mysterious, sultry, intelligent, almost unattainable. God, Ryan couldn't resist a challenge. And Jade Maguire screamed, "Look, but don't touch," a challenge no man could resist.

To his eternal shame, he wanted her in spite of knowing what she'd done. Wanted her with instant avarice and a healthy dose of anger. He wanted her under him, crying for mercy even as she cried out in passion and begged him to take her.

He'd never felt the heady mix of passion and anger before. Never understood its power, though he'd heard of it affecting other men.

Now he got it. It was nearly painful to be in the same room with a woman he'd desired on sight, but who'd swindled a valuable family heirloom from a helpless elderly woman.

Well, he could concede, his grandmother was not exactly *helpless*. She had a steel spine beneath her high-necked blouses—which made it even more imperative for him to get the painting back as soon as possible. The elderly woman was so embarrassed at having been tricked by the deceitful con artist that she'd refused to bring the police in on the case. She'd also forbidden him to tell Grandfather she'd let the painting be stolen. She'd concocted some story about it being on loan for an exhibit to keep the old man from asking any questions. She was relying on Ryan to bring it back before she could get caught.

"I can't tell you how pleased we are that *Architectural Digest* is going to devote an article to the construction of our fair city," Mamie said, interrupting his heated thoughts about the woman across the room.

The article. The reason Ryan was getting the red-carpet treatment here in Savannah. What perfect timing that he'd come here for an annual meeting, after being solicited to write a piece for the journal. He'd kill three birds with one stone.

The conference. The article. And the thief.

"Savannah has paved the way for other cities to save their historic treasures," he replied, completely in earnest. "Anyone who wants to preserve treasured buildings of the past would look to your city as a fine example."

The pudgy woman preened and not very subtly smoothed her hand over the low, tight neckline of her unattractive, fluffy green dress. Very tight. Very low cut. The wares were nearly spilling out, which was apparently what she wanted.

Ryan stiffened ever so slightly and took a small step back. His stance grew a bit more formal as he sent out a silent message that he hoped she'd get. He didn't want to have to flat-out turn her down and risk alienating the woman who owned the inn he'd be sleeping in tonight. Particularly because he imagined she had keys to all the rooms.

He had a sudden mental flash of a fleshy woman creeping into his bed in the dead of night. Talk about your basic nightmares. He'd had flings with older women—his university guidance counselor came to mind—but never *decades* older.

Then the picture in his oversexed brain changed, and it wasn't the proprietress face he imagined entering his room in the dark of night. He saw the thief— Jade—lovely and deceptive. Graceful and conniving. Intoxicating and completely ruthless.

The image of her dark black hair against his white sheets made him gulp a big mouthful of his drink.

"Are you all right, Mr. Stoddard?" Mamie asked as he coughed a bit into his fist.

"Fine," he murmured. "Just...went down the wrong way."

Everything about this situation had gone down the wrong way, from the minute his grandmother had told him she'd been robbed. First, tracking the wrong J. Maguire from Savannah, he'd wound up meeting the younger sister, Jenny, up in New York. He'd realized within hours that she wasn't the right woman. Thankfully, he'd only taken her out to lunch once. So she wouldn't have had any reason to mention him to her sister.

The second detective he'd hired—a *better* one—had found Jade, and his grandmother had confirmed the description. Ryan had taken the information and come to Savannah determined, in charge, using the cover of the convention and the article to get where he wanted to be—close to her.

Everything had gone fine. Right up until the moment he'd actually seen the woman he was after.

He could be in over his head with this one. It was somehow exciting, rather than disturbing, to imagine the sexy brunette sneaking into his room. Trying her tricks on him, creeping in to take something that belonged to him. Taking *him.*

He forced the traitorous thought away. Yes, she was damned attractive and he had to clench his fists to remind himself he had to *trick* her. Not *take* her.

Unfortunately.

"Well, if you need any help getting around," Mamie said, not noticing his distraction, "I'd be more than happy to help you in *any* way." She drew her hand to her throat again, flashing a big chunky rock on her ring finger and tapping her collarbone with the tip of her red-tinted fingernail.

Not on your best day, lady.

Since she hadn't gotten the nonverbal hint, he gave her a broader one. "I'm also enjoying getting to meet some of the beautiful *young* women of your city."

That seemed to get through. The woman was twenty years his senior, at least, with a husband dangling around here somewhere, probably downing drinks wondering how he was going to pay for her next party. Not to mention her next diamond.

"Well, there's no shortage of those." This time Mamie's smile was somewhat forced.

"What about her?" Ryan asked, nodding toward Jade, who stood talking with an older woman in a Southern-belle ball gown.

Mamie's mouth stiffened even more. "Jade Maguire. She can show you some things, all right. She owns one of those trashy tour guide companies that prey on out-of-towners who like to be scared out of their wits with silly ghost stories at night."

Nothing he hadn't known. The private detective he'd ordered to track down the *right* J. Maguire had sent a file on Jade's company, *Stroll Savannah*, which had become one of the most popular tourist traps since she'd opened it a few years ago.

He knew where she lived. Where she'd gone to school. What she liked to drink and when she liked to eat. Who she employed. Who she dated—nobody, really, which had been a surprise. When she traveled and where she went.

He'd been prepared for everything. Everything except how beautiful she was.

"You can find *better* tour guides," Mamie said.

The biting tone in the woman's voice was a surprise. Then again, he imagined a woman who looked like

Jade got a lot of jealous responses from overweight, aging society matriarchs. He was about to put the woman in her place, some unexpected instinct making him want to defend Jade, a woman he personally had hated for weeks. But before he could do so, Mamie continued.

"Her father was just an Irish bartender."

"So she's not a native of the city?"

Mamie shrugged, then grudgingly conceded, "She's actually part of a long lineage of Savannians. On her mother's side. Her father's name was Maguire, but her mother's maiden name was *Dupré*." The woman leaned close, looking around to ensure she wasn't being overheard. "Some of those Duprés…well, they're not quite the *purest* family line, if you know what I mean."

He didn't. And for some reason, though he should want to gather more ammunition to use against Jade, he resented the woman's snide tone and didn't ask for details.

"The party's going well."

She frowned at the change of subject, looking disappointed that he hadn't taken the bait. Why hadn't he? *Stupid*. That'd been a stupid move. But he somehow couldn't find it within himself to regret it.

"I suppose." Then she put out her dark-tinted bottom lip in a small pout. "Are you going to be moving to the Winter Garden House tomorrow? You're sure we can't convince you to stay?"

Ryan shook his head. "Sorry. I must spend some time at all the inns I'll be writing about."

Not to mention the fact that Jade Maguire's tour company capped off their nighttime haunted history tour with a visit to the famous Winter Garden inn. Since he'd paid one of her employees to call in sick tomorrow night, he knew damn well who'd be leading the tour.

It was almost too easy luring the tigress into his den.

Hell, she was making it even *easier* because she'd been looking at him all night. Giving him these intense stares, studying him.

Ryan was used to the stares of women. Under normal circumstances, this woman's interest would have gotten exactly the kind of reaction he'd always had to a beautiful, seductive female. Instant heat. Hot pleasure. The kind of crazy passionate relationship he'd enjoyed more than a few times in his life. The kind that had kept him from settling down to anything more permanent—much to his grandmother's dismay.

Grandmother didn't believe he wasn't secretly interested in marriage, kids and all the suburban crap the women she introduced him to seemed to want. And he didn't want to force her to admit he didn't possess the love-at-first-sight gene that had downed so many of his family members.

So the least he could do for evading her marriage traps was reclaim a family treasure.

He hadn't realized, though, until he'd set eyes on Jade, that the job might be so very enjoyable. Getting her naked, helpless and at his mercy might prove to be fun. He just had to keep reminding himself this was a mission. Business, not pleasure.

Though, honestly, if some pleasure happened into the equation, he didn't think he'd protest too much.

2

"YOU'VE BEEN WATCHING ME," a smooth voice said, low and melodic and hinting at other words, more sultry words, that he'd rather not say in public.

Ryan Stoddard. God, he'd come right up to her. Jade hadn't expected him to make the first move.

"You've been watching *me*," she countered, sipping her drink and not turning around. She closed her eyes and did a rapid one-to-ten count to gain control. She couldn't believe he'd eased around the crowd and snuck up on her while she'd been watching Tally work her magic with the rich businessman.

On the positive front, she'd only been here an hour and already the object of her revenge scheme had approached her. She was getting almost too good at this clandestine thing. Though, she had to admit, the ability to be noticed in a crowd had come in handy on some of her treasure-hunting jaunts. Particularly with the *male* targets.

He moved closer. The fabric of his trousers brushed her bare legs, which were revealed well above the knee in a short jet-black beaded cocktail dress that didn't quite suit the dress code tonight. The contact stirred her, made something lurch within her.

"We've been watching each other," he admitted, his voice closer now. Close enough for her to feel his breath on her neck.

Goose bumps rose there. Goose bumps, for heaven's sake, as if she hadn't been practicing this man/woman/sex thing since before she'd grown breasts. Every Dupré woman knew about seduction, just as every Dupré woman knew about the family history and the many ways to curse someone in the old language.

"If it makes you feel better to think so, go ahead."

He chuckled, obviously not fooled by her cool tone. How could he be when her whole body was practically arching toward him, shifting with imperceptible need? Was the warmth she felt caused by the hot summer night or by his nearness?

Or by her own anxiety about what she planned to do with this man very, *very* soon?

"You look wicked in that dress."

Nothing subtle about this man.

"Compared to the other ladies in their pastels and jewel tones, I mean."

She knew darn well he hadn't been talking about the color of her dress. He'd meant her. That *she* looked wicked.

Wicked as in *hot*. Not *bad*.

Which was good, since she didn't want him to know yet just how bad she could be. Particularly when she had payback on her mind.

"You mean I'm dressed inappropriately?" she asked, smoothing her hand across the front of her dress in a provocative stroke.

His response—a laugh—caught her by surprise. When she frowned, he quickly explained. "My landlady tried the exact same move on me not ten minutes ago. Trust me, it works much better on you than it did on someone whose chins almost meet her cleavage."

Having no liking for Mamie Brandywine—who'd

been downright rude to Jade's mother on more than one occasion—Jade smiled, and forgave him for his laughter. "You should see her in a bathing suit."

He visibly shuddered.

"I'm sure she'd be happy to join you in the spa."

"I'd rather be boiled in oil."

"Warm oil. I'm sure she could arrange that, too. She's, uh, rather *fond* of her male guests."

He raised an offended hand to his chest and shook his head. "You mean, it's not just me? She wasn't bowled over by my manly charms and extraordinary looks?"

Jade couldn't help it. She let out a little snort, amused by his self-deprecating tone. "Don't flatter yourself. She'd be trying to get Attila the Hun naked in the hot tub if he were here. I think that's why she had it installed."

"I don't think the two of them would fit." Then he added, "And if she's used it a lot for her 'dates,' I think I'd better make a mental note—no hot tub for me."

Against her will, Jade reacted to his good humor. She liked his snappy comebacks and quick mind. Then she remembered what had gotten them on the subject of Mamie Brandywine to begin with. "By the way, I was *not* making a come-hither move."

"You weren't?" he asked, his voice growing husky. "You mean, you didn't deliberately move your open hand across your breasts, until your nipples got hard against your pretty black dress?"

She gasped. How on earth did he think he could get away with speaking to a complete stranger, in *public*, like that?

He didn't even pause. "You didn't intentionally run your thumb under the neckline, inviting a man to imag-

ine the way your skin tastes?" Then he lifted her hand
and laced his fingers through hers. "Not to mention
your long fingernails just barely scraping across your
skin, dipping between your breasts, inviting him to an-
ticipate what it would be like to kiss you there, lick the
hollow of your throat, then follow the path your own
hand had taken?" He gave her a wicked look, silently
daring her to lie. "*None* of it was intentional?"

Jade froze, her legs turning to lead and her lips parting to suck in breath. Lord have mercy, what had she
gotten herself into here? This man used words the way
an artist used paint. He'd woven a spell around her, as
heavy and intoxicating as one of Lula Mae's brews.
And he'd done it with only his voice.

She suddenly began to wonder if she'd made a very
serious miscalculation.

Because instead of being the seducer, she was very
much afraid she might end up the one seduced.

HE HAD HER. HE KNEW IT at that moment. The cool, confident goddess had turned into a stammering high
school girl.

Women. Unbelievable what kind of verbal B.S. they
fell for.

Though, he hadn't entirely been B.S.'ing. He'd had
to force his voice to remain steady as he'd seduced her
with words because, in truth, he'd meant everything
he'd said. Though, in any other situation, he'd never
have been so outrageous and suggestive with a woman
he'd just met. The women he knew were the same cool,
mature businesspeople he interacted with every day.

Not like her. Not like Jade. The kind who had him
thinking of nothing but what her curves looked like
under that black dress, how her mouth would taste,

how her hair would feel spread out across his naked chest.

How she stole from your own family, asshole!

Yeah. That, too. This hot seductress used her Southern act to convince others she was intelligent, respectable, in control.

And honest.

She'd fooled his very astute grandmother into thinking she was a professional restorer of valuable art. That's how she'd conned Grandmother out of the beautiful Jules LeBeuf portrait. The elderly woman would never have handed over the painting, done by a lesser-known French Impressionist in the 1850s, without believing it was in good hands.

Such pretty hands. Such soft hands. Such talented hands…most especially when it came to things like picking locks. Or pockets.

"You seem to think you know how to charm a woman. I suppose you've had a lot of experience?"

Her voice was a little shaky. She was obviously still affected by the outrageous things he, a stranger, had just said to her. But there was also a hard note, as if she had her back up for some reason.

"No more than any other man," he said, lifting his shoulders in what he hoped looked like self-deprecation. Then he quirked a brow. "That's what I'm supposed to say, right? So I don't appear too confident?"

"I don't think that's possible. You wear your confidence like some men wear their clothes."

"Attractive and in good taste, I hope?"

"I was thinking more along the lines of flashy and overdone," she replied, though her insult lacked the punch she'd probably intended.

"Should I go away?" he asked, knowing the answer.

She shook her head. "So far you haven't done anything completely unredeemable."

No, she didn't want him to go away. She was still wrapped in the cozy, intimate place they'd stumbled into here in the midst of all these people. And she was still as affected as he was. He just hid it better.

Jade began rubbing her hand up and down one bare arm, as if warming herself. But the noticeable goose bumps on her skin weren't caused by cold—the room was sweltering.

No, their interaction was putting her entire body on high alert. But before he could call her on it, her attention was diverted by someone who paused to speak to her.

Ryan watched quietly, silently admitting that he, too, was on high alert. He tried to analyze it. This hot flush of awareness and excitement couldn't be brushed off as righteous indignation or the culmination of a couple of weeks' buildup. Being truly honest about it, he believed he'd have reacted just as strongly to Jade Maguire if this really had been a chance meeting at a party.

Ryan had known a lot of women over the years, and been involved with his fair share. Probably more than his fair share. He'd even come close to commitment, getting engaged to a Manhattan lawyer he'd met at a cocktail party a few years ago. But he hadn't been able to go through with it, and neither had she. They'd both figured out that while the two of them made a picture-perfect couple, they'd never shared the kind of deep, soul-stirring passion a marriage should have.

His grandmother would probably never believe it, and she'd laugh in his face if he told her. But one of the main reasons Ryan had never settled down—never even tried to feign interest in any of the women she, his mother and his sister had set him up with over the years—was because of the example his family had set. His grandparents were mad for each other. Ditto his parents. And Jane, his younger sister, was deeply in love with her husband.

Though he didn't believe he could fall madly in love at first sight—as other members of his family claimed to have—he did think he was capable of real love.

And he *wanted* it.

His family had set a high standard. Deep inside, he knew he couldn't settle for less. Unfortunately, so far Ryan had never felt that way about anyone. Never lost his mind, lost his heart or even lost control of his emotions over a single female he'd ever met.

Which made his instant reaction to this one that much more surprising. And intriguing. He'd never felt as sparking with energy, as...*alive* with a woman as he did in the brief time he'd known Jade Maguire.

Before he could take any longer to wonder about it, they were interrupted by Mamie Brandywine. "Well, here you are," she said to Ryan, giving him a broad smile. Then she turned her attention to Jade. "I'm surprised to see *you* here. This isn't your usual crowd, is it?" She shook her head and tsked. "And I must protest, you're monopolizing our special guest."

No love lost between those two, he'd already figured out by Mamie's earlier comments, so he wasn't exactly surprised by the woman's hard tone. Jade responded with a lazy smile and amused silence that practically dared Mamie Brandywine to push harder.

Mamie didn't push. And Ryan's interest in Jade went up another notch. *A woman with a lot of nerve, that one.*

Rather than losing the staring contest with Jade, Mrs.

Brandywine backed down and turned her attention back to Ryan. She took his arm, saying, "I want you to meet someone. The owner of the inn we were discussing is right over there."

The Winter Garden. The inn where he'd be staying, starting tomorrow. He did *not* want Jade to know he'd be there. It might be enough to make her suspicious when he put Plan B into action.

Plan A was to seduce her, get close enough to her and try to get her to reveal something that might lead him to the painting.

Plan B was…well…a little riskier and involved the inn.

And a pair of handcuffs.

"You won't mind if I steal him away, will you, Jade? Surely you can find some other way to amuse yourself," Mamie said. "There are lots of men here who might find your little ghost stories interesting."

"Of course there are, and I'm sure you've…*met*… them all," Jade said, her smile never fading. All three of them knew her hesitation had been intentional.

Mamie stiffened as Jade continued pleasantly, "By the way, you do look *lovely* in your dress. How funny, I think Auntie Lula Mae has a stuffed dead bird in exactly that color."

Ryan bit the inside of his cheek to hide a laugh as his landlady's heavily made-up face went a few shades paler. From behind Jade, he saw another woman—the one in the hoop skirts who'd been talking with Jade earlier—listening intently. At Jade's cutting insult, the woman grabbed her middle and laughed so hard she almost dropped her drink.

Okay, so at least one other woman here liked the sultry brunette.

Before the offended inn owner could muster up a suitable retort, she was joined by a middle-aged man wearing a slightly faded black tuxedo. His horn-rimmed glasses covered a weary-looking pair of eyes.

Those eyes lit up when the man spied Jade. "Jade, you look wonderful!"

For the first time since he'd joined her, Ryan saw the young woman loosen up and smile with genuine fondness. She stood on her tiptoes and kissed the man on the cheek. "Hello, Uncle Henry."

Ah, more relations. Another thing about the South, everybody was related to everybody.

"Your mama got off on her cruise all right? Gee, honey, I was so sorry to miss the wedding."

Mamie Brandywine's stiff mouth said she, for one, was *not* sorry to have missed the wedding.

"She's fine. Having the time of her life, I imagine."

"Better on the high seas than here causing trouble," Mamie interjected. "Though I hope the other wives on board keep their husbands close at hand."

Jade's jaw stiffened and her face flushed red. For the first time, it appeared the obnoxious Mamie Brandywine had scored a hit.

She opened her mouth to retort. But before she could do so, Ryan interceded. "If you'll excuse us, we were just about to dance."

Then, not taking no for an answer, he plucked Jade's drink out of her hands and put it on the tray of a passing waiter. Taking a strong hold of her arm, he led her away, heading toward the dance floor, feeling her fury and resistance with every step.

He should have known better than to think she'd let it go. After only a half-dozen steps, she planted her feet and refused to proceed.

So, instead of allowing the fireworks, he did the only thing he could think of.

He kissed her.

JADE HAD BEEN PREPARED for reasoning, an apology, a joke, anything a man might typically do to calm down an angry woman.

But not this. Not this amazing kiss. Not his mouth teasing the corner of hers, then moving over until their lips met completely. He wasn't holding her close, wasn't restraining her in any way. Yet she still felt completely touched. Held. Embraced. By nothing but his lips.

Somehow, she couldn't even bring herself to care that she was standing in a crowd of people allowing a complete stranger to kiss her. Maybe because it felt so incredibly good, an unexpected gift of pleasure like suddenly feeling the sun on her face during what had been a cloudy day.

He didn't try to deepen the kiss, merely playing with her mouth, letting her lips savor the pleasure of his as they shared breaths and as her anger eased away. Finally, after what seemed like forever, he pulled away and looked at her.

She couldn't say a word, could only stare up at him in confusion, her mouth falling open but no sound coming out. He touched her chin with his index finger, pushed her mouth closed and whispered, "Dance with me."

Then he slipped his arm around her waist and led her onto the crowded floor. Like Moses parting the Red Sea, his mere presence made people step to the sides, moving away to create room for them. He nodded his thanks, gave polite smiles and left the women groveling in his wake while the men lifted their chins in annoyance.

Good lord, no wonder Jenny had fallen for this man. He'd completely taken over this society party, as if he belonged. As if he'd been born here and could trace his ancestry back several generations—as Jade could—instead of coming from some cold northern city where people didn't know their neighbors' names, much less their great-grandparents'.

"I'm afraid I don't know the latest steps to elevator music," he whispered as their bodies moved together and began to sway. "But I don't think rigid as a board is the right position."

Jade couldn't prevent a tiny laugh from escaping between her clenched teeth. She had, indeed, been rigid and inflexible, still trying to deal with his words, with that kiss. Not to mention his...*presence*. That was the only word to describe it.

He was so unlike any of the men she'd known or dated. His looks were one thing—good looks were easy to find, and also easy to forget if they weren't backed up with personality. But this man had more than the looks and the personality. It was his aura, his power, his self-confidence, that she found nearly irresistible. He commanded respect. And, she suspected, he knew how to give it in return.

Almost against her will, she relaxed against him, the contact causing both instant pleasure and instant tension.

Bad idea.

His body was long, thick and hard.

All over?

She thrust the naughty thought away, lest it distract her once again from her mission. It didn't help, particularly when she realized that if things went as planned, she'd be finding out his secrets—size and all—in a very short while. She nearly shuddered at the thought, remembering how lost she'd been because of a simple kiss.

Maybe you can't do this after all.

Can't, however, was among Jade's least favorite words. It always had been. Nothing made her give something her all as much as being told she couldn't do it.

She *would* do it. Would leave Mr. Smooth quaking and humiliated by the time she got through with him.

Or she'd go down trying.

Go down. The image hit the wicked half of her brain with a vengeance and her legs started to shake again.

Stop it, Jade. Get your mind out of his pants!

All the muscles in her body tensed as she strove for control.

"You're stiff again," he said.

"Stiff. Yes," she murmured, still more than a little unsettled with the undeniably erotic direction her thoughts had taken. Pretty bad to have those kind of thoughts about a man she'd hated before laying eyes on him. It had obviously been *way* too long since she'd had sex.

"Relax. You're all tense because of silly Mrs. Brandywine."

"She deserves to be taken down a peg."

"Wasn't it enough for her to be told that her dress looked like a dead bird?" he asked, a twinkle in his eye.

Jade bit her lip, still unable to believe she'd given in and done exactly what she'd sworn to Tally she wouldn't do. The cutting insult had just fallen off her lips, as naturally as could be. She hadn't given it a moment's thought.

"I guess I do have a bit of my mother in me." Then, remembering what Mamie had said, went on to add, "Mrs. Brandywine hates my mother because Mama's first husband was Mamie's high school boyfriend."

"High school. Long time to hold a grudge."

Jade shrugged. "Long grudges aren't unusual down here. Go bring up the Civil War to some of the old-timers."

"No, I'm not that daring," he said with a laugh.

The small band segued into yet another slow, dreamy melody. As they moved together, his leg slid between hers in a move too perfectly aimed to be acci-dental. She gasped at the contact, not expecting him to be so deliberately bold again so soon.

He tried to claim otherwise. "I'm not the best dancer."

She sucked in a shaky breath. "You're doing okay." Then she repositioned herself and shot him a warning look, telling him she knew he'd done it intentionally. "But don't try it again."

He didn't even apologize. Not that she'd expected him to. Instead he remained just out of reach, a breath separating them, so only the fronts of their bodies touched from shoulder to hip. The near-contact was driving her out of her mind. Her earlier curiosity re-turned in full force.

Long. Thick. Hard. And more…*hot.*

He radiated heat and energy, from the intensity in his green eyes to the strength in his hands to the breadth of his impossibly wide shoulders. The man screamed masculine, sexual, powerful and untamed.

And she was really going to try to tame him? No, not tame him, *punish* him?

Yet another feeling of uncustomary uncertainty

flashed in her brain, which really irked her. She hadn't been uncertain about anything related to sex for a long time. Not since deciding to lose her virginity to her college-age neighbor when she'd been in high school.

"Where are you?" he asked softly.

She shook her head and forced a smile and a trill of light laughter. "Right here. Can't you feel me?"

He nodded, slowly, and pulled her tighter. A little too tight for propriety's sake. Warmth built inside her. She felt a trickle of moisture on her upper lip. And elsewhere.

"Has this happened to you before?" He nearly whispered in her ear, his voice husky.

"What?"

"Something this instant?"

He didn't have to elaborate. They both knew what he was talking about.

She answered with complete honesty. "No." Then, because she didn't want him getting too cocky, added, "Not *this* quickly, anyway. I think it usually takes at least a half hour and a glass of wine for me to determine compatibility."

"So, should I be scared or glad that you're drinking soda?"

"How did you know that?" she asked in surprise.

"I've been watching you very closely. All evening. Now, answer the question. Am I not worthy of wine yet?"

She chuckled, unable to resist his teasing expression, though she did worry about how observant he was. "I haven't quite decided yet," she said, needing to regroup and remind herself that the man was a pig and a creep and a despoiler of innocent young girls. Supposedly.

Jenny wouldn't lie.

No, her sister wouldn't outright lie. But she was something of a drama queen, which suited her desire to be an actress. Her tendency to exaggerate was well-known in the family, as well as to the Savannah police. Jade had gotten her sibling out of several scrapes, even stepping in to keep Mama in the dark when Jenny's outrageous behavior got her into serious trouble.

But she couldn't have lied about this. Jade had even seen a picture of them together. Though it had been poor quality, so his face was slightly blurred, she believed this was the man who'd been in the picture. He'd had his arm laid casually over Jenny's shoulders, she looking exquisitely happy—as any woman would when being held by a man who looked like pure sex wrapped in an Armani suit.

Jenny hadn't lied. Maybe he hadn't *meant* to hurt her. Probably he hadn't, given that even during their very brief acquaintance, she'd already realized that though he was a flirtatious, sexy playboy who turned on the charm with anyone female and breathing, he didn't seem the type to abuse his power over women.

Unfortunately, he'd turned that charm on a young woman unable to handle it, and broken her heart. He was a grown man, thirty at least. Old enough to know better than to mess with a twenty-one-year-old kid. So whether he'd done it intentionally or not, Ryan Stoddard had to pay.

He *would* pay. And he would definitely know better by the time Jade finished with him.

"Now, we haven't been properly introduced, have we?" he whispered, his breaths brushing her hair and tickling her ear. "Your name is Jade?"

She cleared her throat and replied, "Yes. Jade." She didn't offer her last name.

"I'm Ryan Stoddard."

Definitely no mistake then. A stab of regret dashed through her as an unspoken wish that he might *not* be the rotten man she'd thought he was—that she'd made some colossal mistake and some other amazing architect had shown up at the party tonight—disappeared. She looked into his eyes, so clear and honest-looking. Any woman could get lost in them. Including a very young, impressionable woman.

She was once again forcibly reminded of the reason for tonight's interaction. Revenge.

The crazy, sexy spell she'd been under dissipated. She finally managed to dig deep and reinforce her wavering determination by picturing Jenny in this man's arms. That mental picture hurt. Badly. Maybe not for the right reasons, but it worked anyway. She didn't pause to evaluate those reasons, sensing they could be based more on jealousy than family loyalty.

Family loyalty. It was all that really mattered when one grew up as she had. The name Dupré was associated with both power and loss, sadness and ancient scandal. The family had become adept at dealing with whispers and innuendo, envy and tragedy, until the Duprés had become almost a world unto themselves. That world was a safe haven where loyalty and love were valued above all. It was especially comforting to Jade that she was related to so many people here in Savannah.

One thing was sure, the Dupré women had withstood worse than playboys like Ryan Stoddard.

Back in control at last, Jade widened her lips into the smile perfected by generations of Southern women.

Warm but not effusive. Friendly but not precisely welcoming. With a bit of Dupré woman thrown in—purely seductive.

"Well, welcome to Savannah, Ryan. I'll try my best to make your stay as...*memorable* as possible."

3

FOR THE NEXT HOUR, Jade concentrated on the plan. She put herself as a barrier between Ryan and any of the other women at the party who'd been giving him the eye. Tally, for some reason, seemed to want to help. She ran interference once or twice, including saying something to Mamie Brandywine that made the woman's face turn as red as her long, fake fingernails.

While standing in a shadowy corner, nibbling on canapés and sipping her drink, she leaned forward and touched him as often as she could. Laughed at the appropriate moments. Batted her eyelashes like a stupid twit and all in all did whatever one did to try to attract a man. It had been a long time since she'd wanted to.

She didn't want to consider whether or not she'd have been trying to attract Ryan Stoddard if she didn't have to bring him down. Because the answer would probably be *yes*.

"So how do you like our town?" She pursed her lips a bit, inviting him to stare and remember their kiss. "And its people?"

He tilted his head and arched his brow, staring at her mouth for a long moment—as he was meant to. Finally, he shook his head and tightened his jaw before coming up with a reply. "How do you know I'm not from here?"

"I know," she replied, certain she'd affected him. Men—they were all so utterly predictable. She gave him a warm laugh, inviting him to join in a gentle jibe at her hometown. "This is a small town for a modern city."

She didn't bother going into detail about how long her family had lived here, how many local families had ties to hers, and how her great-aunt was the local voo-doo priestess who could name nearly every pure-blooded Savannah resident.

"It's interesting," he said. "Different from New York."

"Are you from there?" she asked, wanting to know more of his background, in case she needed to use it against him. She knew he'd met Jenny in New York City, but wasn't entirely sure that was where he lived.

"Yep. Born and raised. Now I live in Manhattan."

Manhattan. So he probably had money. He carried himself like a man completely comfortable with his finances.

She'd been to New York last month on one of her treasure-hunting trips, when she'd recovered an Impressionist painting from a very nice elderly couple who lived upstate. The painting had already been returned to the original plantation from which it had been stolen during the Civil War. The place now operated as a tourist destination outside the city and they were utterly thrilled to have the portrait back where it belonged.

For a second, she wondered if perhaps she'd spotted Ryan during her trip, and if that was why he'd seemed familiar to her when she'd first seen him tonight. Maybe her subconscious remembered him.

The picture, stupid.

Yeah, the picture of him with Jenny. No, it hadn't been a great one, and she'd only seen it briefly. But it'd obviously made an impression. As did the man.

"Let me know when you decide you want that glass of wine, okay?" he said, eyeing her empty soda cup.

She knew what he meant. It had already been more than half an hour. No wonder he was getting confident. There'd been no hesitation, no doubt in his voice. He thought he had her. Hell, maybe he did. At least for an hour or so.

Until she could get him naked.

"All right," she replied. "But for now, maybe we should just dance again."

"Suits me fine."

Suited her fine, too. Especially because, when they returned to the dance floor, he moved his cheek close to her hair and inhaled. She knew his head was filled with the special orange-blossom-and-almond conditioner Aunt Lula Mae made for her. His murmur of appreciation told her he liked it. He liked *all* of it.

Good. The man was making it incredibly easy. He'd sought her out—she hadn't even had to make a move on him. When he looked back on things later, he'd have to remember that much, at least.

"You truly seem to fit in here," he murmured as the music continued and they moved as carefully as possible amid the crush of people.

"You don't."

He chuckled. "Why not?"

"Blue suit. Genuine smile. Interested look."

"That makes me stand out?"

"Like a June bug in a bowl of rice."

He laughed again, looking down at her, eyes sparkling with interest. Dark green. Long lashed. Crinkled at the corners, probably from casting his wicked smile at any woman old enough to be affected by it.

He's a heart-breaking reprobate! She struggled to remember that as he continued to smile down at her.

"I like Southerners."

"We don't particularly care for you-all."

That made him laugh out loud.

She nibbled her lip, forcing her eyes to focus somewhere over his right shoulder so she wouldn't get caught up again in his good humor, wouldn't lose herself in his twinkling eyes and irresistible grin. Maybe dancing hadn't been such a good idea. Hard to remember silly things like family honor and vengeance when being held closely by a man as fine as this one.

"Honesty. I like that in a woman."

Well, darlin', you're not gonna like me very much, then.

"So tell me, how can I make myself fit in?"

"Got a few million dollars lying around?"

He shook his head.

"Genteel impoverished, but able to trace your lineage back to before the war?"

"Which war?"

She raised a brow and gave him a wounded look. "Whichever do you think?"

Their eyes met and she saw the laughter in his. He'd been teasing her, just as she'd been teasing him.

"I'm afraid I'm an Irish-English-German mutt," he replied with a mournful-sounding sigh. "Can't trace my roots further back than Ellis Island, for the most part."

"But I bet you have good taste in beer. Irish, English, German?"

He nodded, still looking amused.

"Unfortunately, that doesn't get you in with this crowd."

"How about with you?"

"Are you offering to buy me a beer?" she asked, leaping on the opening he'd provided. The time had come to get him alone. Now—before her defenses dropped even further and she forgot she wasn't allowed to like this man. "I doubt they serve it here."

"I have some in the fridge up in my room."

Ooh, cutting right to the chase. Trying to get her up to his room. How incredibly easy he was making this. And his smooth way of trying to get her alone reinforced her certainty that he was the creep her sister made him out to be, even though he'd been nothing but charming and friendly—if a bit flirtatious—all evening.

"I could meet you on the back patio for a cold one."

Okay, so he *wasn't* trying to get her to his room. She didn't know whether to feel relieved or disappointed.

She'd thought through several scenarios. The original one had involved his hotel room, a bedpost, her long red scarf and a wide-open door. Because he'd moved to the Medford House, she'd have to modify things a bit.

But the scarf was still included.

"How do you know I'm the beer-drinking type?" she asked as he waited for her answer.

His expression screamed confidence, as if he knew all there was to know about her after an hour of conversation.

"Let me tell you what I've figured out about you."

She smirked, daring him to be accurate.

"You've been nursing ginger ale all evening. Before I rescued you, you'd done nothing but look at the paintings, the furniture and that old necklace. You didn't return one glance at one of the rich guys who'd probably love to invite you to bathe in champagne back at their pampered palaces."

"Champagne bath? Sounds ticklish," she retorted, though the mental image created a surge of warmth low in her body.

He ignored her. "Your foot was tapping with suppressed energy and your fingers clenched and released about thirty times a minute."

"You were watching me that long, hmm?"

He didn't try to deny it. "You had my complete attention the moment I became aware of your existence."

There was a note of intensity, almost a growl in his voice, which surprised her. Again she wondered, briefly, if she'd ever met him before, perhaps on one of her trips to track down and retrieve artifacts stolen from local families during the war.

But she knew she hadn't. This was one man she would never have been able to forget.

"Your face, your mouth, your eyes, your body, they were all saying one thing," he continued, uncaring of the open ears surrounding them on the dance floor.

Take me?

"Bored."

That, too.

"Bored enough to want to do something different." His voice lowered, and there was an unmistakably suggestive tone in it. "Maybe something crazy. Which is why I decided to shock you out of your boredom during our initial conversation."

Oh, yeah, their initial conversation. The one that had included mention of her nipples and breasts, both of which were still aching as their bodies brushed against each other.

"I'm still not sure I've forgiven you."

"I don't think I asked for forgiveness."

Again that confidence. That suggestive—not salacious—tone. He was a self-assured man who'd noted their instant attraction and was acting on it without games, without the typical steps of flirtation. She liked that about him. Damn, she liked him more and more the longer she remained in his arms.

"Are you sure you're not a P.I. or something? You're pretty good at watching people," she said.

Her tone was teasing, though she was a teensy bit worried. If she didn't know for certain he was an architect, she might have thought the P.I. thing was nearer to the truth. The man was incredibly observant!

"You're very interesting to watch," he said, his voice low and only for her ears. "Fascinating." Then he lightened up. "Besides, it beats watching the white-haired guy with the ruffled shirt trying to look down the blouse of every cocktail server here."

She followed his glance. "Mr. Sherman. Disgusting, but harmless, especially since his wife tried to castrate him back in the seventies."

He stopped dancing, nearly stumbling on his own feet. His eyes were wide and she merely shrugged. The story was an old one.

"You're serious?"

"Why do you think none of the servers have slapped his face? Everyone feels sorry for the limp old thing."

He shook his head, drawing her close again to continue the dance. "What about the couple over by the buffet table? He looks thirty years too young to be her husband. I thought she was his mother until I saw them kiss on the dance floor."

Jade glanced over, unable to hide a frown of disgust when she saw the couple. "The latest divorced matron with her rebound boy toy."

"That kind of thing happens in the rich crowd even in the South?" He sounded truly surprised.

"Obviously you haven't seen or read The Book."

"The Book?"

"The tell-all novel that changed the image of Savannah in print and on film."

He nodded. "Ahh. *Midnight in the Garden of Good and Evil.*"

"Here, we just call it The Book."

"Okay. And actually, I have seen the movie. I assumed it was fiction."

"Some was. But not the eccentricities of the city's residents."

He shrugged, looking neither surprised nor disappointed. "It fits. Eccentricities, beautiful homes, fine things." He stared into her face, studying her eyes, her hair, her cheekbones. Jade resisted the urge to lick her lips, wondering if they were still as glossy red as they'd been when she'd touched up her lipstick earlier.

"I like looking at fine things," he murmured.

She sucked in a breath. The way he said the word *fine* made her shiver deep inside, as if he'd examined her, studied her, and declared her as lovely and desirable as a perfect piece of art.

God, what deceptive things come in pretty packages. Because she wasn't fine. She wasn't being honest. She wasn't *anything* he thought her to be.

For a brief moment, she wished they'd met under different circumstances. If Jenny had never mentioned Ryan Stoddard. If she'd never seen the man's picture—which had enraged Jade even more, considering how irresistible he'd be to a vulnerable twenty-one-year-old. If only...

If only there'd been a big mistake and he wasn't the man she'd sworn revenge on.

But he was. And it was time to get on with it.

"Okay, Ryan. I'll have that beer with you."

RYAN LEFT THE BALLROOM of the old mansion, telling Jade he'd meet her outside in fifteen minutes. She gave him a measured look, then nodded her agreement and stepped out of his arms. He'd had to stand there on the dance floor for a moment, to calm his pulse, to evaluate what he was doing, to make sure he wasn't about to make a mistake.

There was something so intriguing about the woman. Her strength, her charm. The way she stood her ground when surrounded by catty women whose dislike probably stemmed from jealousy more than anything else.

She seemed above it, somehow, not rising to it except for that one moment with Mamie. But even then, she'd regained her cool head pretty quickly.

He didn't know why, but he had a strong sense of misgiving about how the evening was progressing. He was supposed to be the hunter. So why was he suddenly feeling hunted?

"You're imagining things," he told himself. Things were going perfectly. It was only his overactive imagination—and overheated sex drive—that needed to be brought under control.

Unfortunately, someone else overheard. "Imagining things? No, you're not."

Ryan looked up and saw the woman in the hoopskirted ball gown who'd been talking to Jade earlier. She should have looked ridiculous, but somehow, her innate grace made the silly dress work. At least in this setting.

"Tally Jackson," the woman said, extending her hand for a limp, ladylike handshake.

Ryan took it and introduced himself.

"Now, were you thinking you were imagining ghosts?"

Ryan raised a brow.

"You mentioned something about imagining it?"

"No, sorry, I was mumbling to myself."

She tsked. "Best be careful of that. Here in Savannah, you never know when one of your little quirks might end up in the pages of a *book*."

He grinned, having been forewarned by Jade about what book she probably meant.

"I just assumed you saw the ghost," the woman said.

"Ghost?"

"Well, Savannah *is* the most haunted city in the U.S. Oh, this house isn't spectacularly haunted, mind you. Not like the Lowe or the Winston house. But there have been a few occasions when guests swore they heard the sound of a man crying."

"A man?" He raised a disbelieving brow. Ryan didn't bother to hide the sarcasm from his voice, being well used to ghost stories about old buildings like these. "Are you sure you don't mean a poor spurned mistress or a child lost at a tragically young age?"

Tally didn't take offense. "No, no, definitely a man. Some say it was the millionaire who owned the house back at the turn of the century, crying over the woman he loved, who married another." Then she pointed to the curved staircase leading to the upper floors and bedrooms. "He hanged himself from that very banister on Christmas Eve, 1904."

Ryan looked up, wondering if he was supposed to shiver or shudder or feel someone walking over his grave.

None of the above. It was only a staircase. Stairs.

Banister. A normal, sweeping, curved staircase built so often in neoclassical mansions like these. The story was probably one of the dozens made up by con artists like Jade Maguire who made their living scaring the tourists, just like Mamie had said.

"Guess Christmas wasn't very merry that year," he replied with a rueful smile.

"You don't believe me?" Tally said.

"I'm certainly not calling you a liar," he said, trying to end the conversation gracefully."

Tally obviously heard the placating note in his voice and knew he was humoring her. "You don't believe in ghosts? Or is it that you don't believe a Southern woman could capture a man's heart so completely, he can never love another?" Her stare was so intense, so piercing, that he knew the question wasn't merely a casual one. Their eyes held for a long moment, hers asking questions. Before she could voice them, he beat her to the punch.

"Tell me about Jade Maguire," he countered, knowing that's who the woman meant.

"Touché," she said with a light laugh. "You've caught me. I saw you kiss her and nearly tripped over my hoops."

Considering the width of her hoops, that would have presented an interesting sight. "It was impulse. Trying to prevent her from going back to claw Mamie Brandywine."

Tally nodded, showing her disbelief. "Oh, I'm sure it was entirely selfless."

He couldn't deny it. "I won't say I didn't enjoy it...."

She laughed aloud. "Good. I'm sure she did, too."

"You're friendly with Jade?"

She nodded. "Her mother is my second cousin.

We've been best friends since childhood. I love Jade like a daughter."

Ryan heard a hint of warning in her voice.

"She seems…fascinating," he said. "Someone I'd like to get to know better."

Tally studied his face, as if gauging the truth of his words. Then she nodded. "Yes, I think you would. But remember, dear boy, you'd better treat her well. The Dupré women…well, let's say we know how to exact revenge if one of us is done wrong."

"Should I be afraid for my life?"

Or just my valuables?

Tally stepped closer and tapped his chest with the end of her fan, the strap of which she had looped around her wrist. "Not if you don't deserve it." Then she smoothed his jacket, tsking as she stared hard at the color. He guessed Jade had been right about the navy blue thing.

"My goddaughter can handle herself. But I shouldn't like to see her hurt, or give her any more reason to stay away from my parties. It's difficult enough to get her to come to events like these."

"Why?"

"Jade loathes these types of things. Her mother's cup of tea, not Jade's. And Patty Jean is a social butterfly. She also thrives on evenings like these as retribution for her side of the family being excluded from society in the old days."

This was getting interesting. "Excluded?"

Tally nodded, obviously as big a gossip as the owner of this inn. But this gossip might help him get inside the head of the woman he was chasing. Learn what made her tick and what buttons he could push, if it came right down to it.

He'd prefer to bring her down legally, but if he had to resort to blackmail, he'd do it.

"Patty Jean's from the Henri Dupré side of the family." She said it like that was supposed to mean something to him.

"Never heard of him."

Tally shrugged. "You wouldn't have, being a northerner. But that side of the family tree includes lots of scandalous branches."

Hmm. Maybe the family tree grew beautiful thieves. That would certainly explain Jade.

"So," Tally continued, "you'd best be careful with Jade. One of the most famous local Duprés is Lula Mae." The woman turned back toward the ballroom, smiling at someone inside.

"Are you trying to tell me something?" Ryan asked, suddenly feeling Tally wasn't a gossip at all. He sensed she'd been in control of this conversation from the very beginning and had given out only a teeny bit of actual information. Because, now that he thought about it, he realized she hadn't revealed much at all. And then, only what she'd wanted to, not what he'd asked for.

"Oh," Tally said, smiling at him over her shoulder. "Not really. Just wanted to warn you not to get on the wrong foot with Jade. Her great-aunt Lula Mae is a voodoo priestess."

She disappeared back into the crowd, leaving Ryan alone in the foyer. "Voodoo priestess, my ass," he mumbled, wondering why these Southerners loved their supernatural nonsense so much. And why Tally Jackson had felt it necessary to warn him about Jade.

Was her warning meant to keep him away from the mysterious brunette? Or to fascinate him even more? Because he had to admit, he was already pretty fascinated. He'd expected someone cold and calculating and instead had found a hot, sultry woman who turned him on right down to his bones.

Even more surprising, he actually liked her. Her wit, her confidence, her comebacks.

Her smile.

"Moron," he muttered aloud, knowing he'd let his defenses down way too quickly.

He needed to put them back up, and pronto. Because he wasn't backing away from Jade one inch. He had a score to settle, a debt he'd soon be calling in. He trusted her about as much as that little black dress covered her sweet figure, and that wasn't much.

As he went up to his room, he heard the trill of his cell phone in his suit pocket. Too late for a business call, and he'd told his friends he'd be unreachable for a week or two. So it had to be family. Probably not his parents, who were at their mountain place for the summer. And almost certainly not his sister, at home with twin four-month-olds.

That left grandmother.

"Hello?"

"Ryan. How are you? Where are you? What's happening?"

Yep. "I'm fine, Grandmother. Everything's fine."

"Have you found her?"

The anxious tone in the old woman's voice reinforced what his mind had been trying to forget during the hours he'd spent being charmed—and attracted—by Jade.

She'd hurt his family.

"I've found her."

The woman waited expectantly, then finally asked, "And?"

"And, I'm on her trail. Here in Savannah."

"Savannah! Oh, goodness, you found her right there in Savannah?"

"It wasn't hard. If you'd only remembered her first name originally, I wouldn't have been distracted by the wrong woman in New York."

His grandmother sniffed. She had been annoyed that he'd wasted time on the wrong Maguire woman, even though she'd been the one who'd given him only the minor lead of an initial for a first name. "The silly little waitress. Yes, yes. But now you've found her, the real McCoy."

"Maguire."

"Of course. What do you think of her?"

He heard a note of expectation in the old woman's voice and wondered if she didn't think him capable of handling someone as devious as Jade. "She's nothing to be afraid of, Grandmother, just a woman with secrets. I'll figure out where she stashed the LeBeuf. But you're sure you don't want to bring the police in on this, now that we know who she is?"

"Absolutely not!" Her voice sounded almost panicked. God love the old thing, so embarrassed at having been tricked.

"All right. I'll handle Jade Maguire."

Definitely handle her.

"She is beautiful, don't you think?" Grandmother said, her tone now more calm.

"Beautiful, yes. But only skin deep."

"And charming."

"Very charming. She'd have to be to swindle you out of your favorite painting."

"Well," Grandmother said, her voice wavering for the first time, "perhaps I was partially at fault…"

"Nonsense. You were robbed. Victims always wonder if they're to blame, but you're *not*. Jade Maguire is."

Though his grandmother sounded as if she wanted to protest, he didn't give her the opportunity. "It's late. Now go to bed, and let me worry about handling our thief."

"You're sure you can handle her? She is quite a handful, isn't she?"

Quite a handful indeed.

"I can handle her grandmother."

"And you won't tip her off! You won't let her know why you're after her. You'll be discreet. You'll just get close to her, spend time with her, stick to her like glue until you can...figure things out."

He smiled, hearing the worrying tone in the wavering voice. "Discreet as can be. I'll get as close to her as possible, then get the information without ever letting her know I'm on to her."

His grandmother's pleased laugh told him he'd provided the correct answer. "Good. And don't let her get away from you. She's slippery. You're going to need to stay close to that woman, day and night."

Day and night. If only his sweet old grandmother knew how very much he longed to stick with Jade day...and especially night. "I've got it under control. Now, good night."

His grandmother gave in with a reluctant sigh. "Good night. Keep your guard up. She's sinful. A man could get lost with a woman like that."

Yes, definitely lost, he thought as he disconnected the call and headed upstairs to his room. A woman like Jade could make any man lose his mind, give in to his senses. She silently cried out to a very basic, primal need he'd long since thought he'd suppressed—desire.

Flat-out, unrelenting want. The kind of hunger that made his mouth go dry and his hands shake.

Damn, what a vulnerable position to be in with a woman so skilled at deception. She was brilliantly skilled at it. As deceptive and seductive as a modern-day Delilah, and just as deadly. Just as dangerous. And his grandmother wanted him to stay *close* to such a creature.

If only she knew what she was asking of him. She wanted him to reach out to a hot flame, risk life and limb with someone who could burn him badly. Someone as adept at lying as she was at seducing, as good at stealing as she was at flirting.

This entire situation required acting without thinking, going on impulse and giving in to emotions he'd gotten used to controlling. That attitude had seen him through all his previous romantic entanglements, including his botched engagement. Not to mention his career, where he'd gained a reputation for a cool head, a steady hand, and a brilliant eye.

So why, suddenly, did he feel blazing hot, wildly off balance and blind when it came to the dangers he was about to face with Jade Maguire?

He didn't know. Almost didn't recognize the feelings in himself. Another thing to blame the woman for. She had him questioning himself in their short acquaintance and he damn sure didn't like it. He hadn't been unsure of himself in a long, long time.

And tonight certainly wasn't the time to start, no matter how the sexy brunette made him feel.

"Enough," he told his reflection in the mirror when he reached his room.

He quickly stripped off his jacket and tie for their meeting in the garden, then, remembering Jade's sticky fingers, he removed one more item from his back pocket.

His wallet.

4

WHILE RYAN WENT TO HIS room to get their beer—a drink for which Jade had no liking but would develop one quickly since it suited her purpose—she went outside to scope out her attack zone. She knew the grounds well. The Medford House was on the list of sites her company, Stroll Savannah, visited during their walking tours of the city. Jade had staff members who did most of the tours these days, but she'd visited the Medford place often enough to remember the layout.

The rear grounds were walled. The once-white wall, whose stones were now a soft milky gray, provided both a visual and a sound barrier from Taylor Square. It also seemed to provide a time barrier that removed this heavily treed back lawn from the modern world where traffic screeched along in present-day Savannah.

Here in the garden, the only concession to the twenty-first century was the spa the owners had added to appeal to their inn customers. She ignored the spa. Too obvious. Too close to the French doors leading into the ballroom. Too yucky, considering their conversation inside about Mamie Brandywine. He'd never feel comfortable enough to, um…get *comfortable* if he thought they could be so easily spotted.

Instead, she moved into the yard, stepping into the

soft grass, walking on her toes so her spike heels wouldn't slip down into the dirt. The ground was moist, the humidity which had hovered over the city throughout the day having misted down onto the lawn as the evening shadows lengthened. The damp turf brushed against her ankles, against her supersensitive skin, and she nearly cooed at the contact. The ballroom had been wickedly hot. Jade would have liked nothing more than to kick off her shoes, walk in the cool grass, and explore the night.

She'd always been something of a creature of the night. Her mother said it was in her blood, that surely there must have been a vampire or two in the New Orleans side of the family. That wouldn't surprise her. Jade had a passion for vampire novels. Not the gooshy ones with lots of blood and bodies, but the romance ones where the vampires actually had sex.

She wouldn't want to be a vampire if she couldn't have sex.

She laughed softly, knowing what her always-striving-to-be-proper mother would think of tonight's adventure, not to mention Jade's own thoughts. She'd be horrified. So it was a good thing she'd gone off on a cruise with her new husband, leaving Jade to take care of Aunt Lula Mae. And this Ryan Stoddard business.

Then she spied the perfect spot for tonight's interlude. "The fountain," she murmured, beelining toward the little corner area on the east side of the property.

It was shaded by willow, oak and magnolia trees, and curtained by loops of gray Spanish moss, which glistened with the same late-night moisture that clung to the grass. Once upon a time, it had probably been a place where ladies took tea in the afternoon and met their lovers late at night.

Unfortunately, though it did a good impersonation of one, the area was no longer a perfectly private and secluded haven. Back in the days of ladies and tea parties, there hadn't been those nice, powerful spotlights on the back corners of the house and on either side of the French doors. They were mostly pointed toward the statue of the general in the center of the lawn. But when the rear lights were turned on, the entire back yard was also well lit. Certainly anyone standing on the porch would have an excellent view of the antique fountain, complete with angels and seraphs, splashing an endless cycle of cool greenish water.

Not to mention anyone standing next to that fountain.

And the lights *would* be on. Right at midnight, when the entire party would come outside to raise a glass to the statue of the general. This grand reopening had been scheduled for his birthday, just so they could make the annual toast.

"Perfect," she murmured as she sat on a stone bench beside the fountain, waiting for Ryan Stoddard.

He'd think they were unseen. And they would be.

"Until the toast," she said with a grin.

"Toast?" a voice said.

Jade quickly schooled her features into a welcoming look, giving Ryan a smile. "What shall we toast to?"

He joined her on the bench, handing her a glass.

"To new acquaintances?"

"To Savannah?"

He thought it over, then lowered his voice suggestively. "How about to a glass of wine and a half an hour?"

She noted the wicked twinkle in his eye, reflected by the tiny lawn lights outlining the fountain and bench area. Not understanding his reference at first, she lifted the glass to her lips. Jade bit back a sigh of resignation and steeled herself against the bitter taste of beer. But what crossed her lips was a fine, heady, full-bodied red wine.

"Mmm." She closed her eyes and swallowed, appreciating the flavor and the warmth. Now she understood what he'd meant by his toast.

"I didn't take you for the beer-drinking type." He sipped his own, then added, "And I think we've officially known each other for more than a half hour now."

She thought about her comments earlier on the dance floor. A half hour and a glass of wine until she could determine if she was attracted to a man. It had taken less than that with *this* man. Not for the first time this evening, she wondered if she might be in over her head.

It didn't matter, even if she was. She owed it to her sister to see this through, no matter how personally uncomfortable it was becoming. And her attraction to her victim was making things *very* uncomfortable.

"You're very sure of yourself." She inhaled the aroma of the wine and sipped again.

"Just determined."

There was that confidence again. That certainty of her—of the situation, of his own charm—both intrigued her and angered her. Because the same charm had been used on a woman much less adept at handling it than Jade.

"I don't know that I needed the half hour," she said, her voice almost a purr as she hid her flash of anger.

"You want me for my wine, hmm?"

"It *is* good."

He nodded his agreement. "Found it in a tiny local grocery store. I figured they'd only carry six-packs and screw-top bottles."

"Savannah takes its food and wine almost as seriously as it takes its history."

Jade sipped again, daring only a small bit more as the stuff was heady. The warmth pervading her wasn't helping to remind her of her purpose. Nor was the hot summer evening, thick with the smells of moss, freshly-mown grass, and the sweet scent of magnolia from the profusion of trees in the yard.

Not to mention his cologne. Or maybe that was just the natural scent of his skin filling her head.

"Spicy," she murmured, taking a deep breath to appreciate all the scents.

"The wine?"

She rested her glass on the bench and looked at him through half-lowered lashes. "The air."

He gave her a quizzical look, then turned his head and closed his eyes. He remained silent for a moment or two, breathing deeply, then nodded. "You're right. Fragrant's not the right word. Spicy. It fits." Then he set his own glass on the ground, and turned slightly to face her. "Both the air…and *you*."

"Me?" she asked with an air of feigned surprise that every Southern girl had learned by her fifth birthday. She didn't need to add the "li'l ole" part to the sentence. The meaning was clear enough.

"Yes, you. Spicy and dark and exotic." His voice was husky and thick, the low, masculine timbre echoing in her ears for a moment longer than it should have.

It wasn't the first time a man had called her exotic. Her thick brown hair, jet-black lashes and chocolate eyes had invited the description before. She'd inherited the looks from her great-great-grandmother, an acclaimed beauty and granddaughter of a slave. She'd been taken as a mistress by a Louisiana planter named Dupré at an Octoroon ball more than a century ago.

Exotic. Suited her bloodline. After all, she had descended from slaves and mistresses. Women who'd shaped their own destinies in spite of what the men in their lives had demanded.

But Jade had never liked the word exotic as much as she did when it came off this man's perfectly shaped lips.

Cool it. Those lips whispered promises that broke your sister's heart!

And, she reminded herself, they were the ones she needed to kiss. Soon. Very soon. Part of the plan, after all. But even as she moved her mouth to his, being the aggressor, she wondered if this was an entirely altruistic kiss.

When their lips met, she realized something.

No. It wasn't.

Then she couldn't think at all. She could only feel. The touch of their mouths—soft, dreamy. The teeny hitch in her throat as they drew a hair's width apart and shared a breath. Then intense pleasure as he moved forward again, capturing her lips and coaxing them apart with smooth, sweet caresses of his tongue.

She moaned, trying to remember what she was doing here. Trying to remember who she was and what she wanted, when all she could focus on was the new place they'd created with the meeting of their mouths.

"You're not what I expected, Jade," he whispered when they drew apart again.

She immediately stiffened and tried to regain her senses and put her thoughts in order—nearly impossible while still under the spell of his kiss.

Finally she managed to say, "Expected? What could you have expected after an evening's acquaintance?"

His eyes shifted slightly and he bent to retrieve his glass. "I meant, when I saw you inside, I'd expected a cool Southern beauty. Not an impulsive woman I'd be kissing in a private garden within a few hours."

She watched his face, gauging the truth of his words. Again, she couldn't help the tiny moment of wonder about just how easy this was. How quickly he'd fallen into her trap.

"You expected cool, and you got hot instead, is that it?" she asked, tilting her head back in pure provocation, inviting him to look at the line of her neck.

He responded. As if reading her mind, he lowered his mouth and pressed one hot, wet kiss to that hollow. His thick hair brushed her face and she couldn't resist raising her hands to tangle her fingers in it.

Then he moved up to kiss her again, his lips still tasting of the wine. The kiss was deeper, harder than before as they both acknowledged the buildup of passion between them.

And suddenly Jade began to wonder if she was really going to be able to go through with her plan after all. Because, somehow, letting this revenge-only seduction turn into a real one seemed altogether too appealing.

RYAN HADN'T KNOWN WHAT he'd find when he came outside into the garden. An armed woman demanding his money? A trickster telling him a sob story and begging him for a way out of some financial trouble?

Certainly not *this*. Certainly not a seductress. God help him, never a wanton, irresistible lover.

He'd fallen right into her web, been totally suckered

by the moonlight on her hair, the way the red wine drenched her lips, darkening them with a seductive moisture until he had to kiss them or go crazy.

She'd tasted amazing. Even better than she had inside, on the dance floor, because this time she'd initiated the kiss. She'd wanted it. Demanded it.

And he'd been more than happy to give it to her.

Now, however, he was finally regaining his senses. He needed to step back, to regroup. To remember who he was and why he was here before he did something stupid like have sex on a public lawn with the woman who'd robbed his helpless old grandmother.

That stiffened his spine. He pulled his mouth away, resisting the urge to inhale one more deep breath of that intoxicating scent she wore, and slid away on the bench. She pulled back, eyeing him through half-lowered lashes. The fullness of her lips nearly pulled him back into another kiss. Nearly.

He resisted the urge by reaching over and thrusting his fist into the cool water of the fountain. "Cool. Feels good on a night this hot. I didn't know what the term *sultry* meant until I came here to Georgia."

She quirked a brow. "We're talking about the weather now? Sultry as in hot and humid?"

Hot, yes. Sultry, yes. And he'd be willing to bet she was more than a little humid after the passionate kiss they'd just exchanged. His body had certainly reacted with sexual predictability, which made his pants uncomfortably tight across his lap.

"Yes, as in hot and humid *weather*."

Her bottom lip curled out in a tiny pout. "My, I think that's the first time I've ever been kissed by a man who then proceeded to talk about the weather." Her curved lips hinted at disappointment, but her eyes were sharp, studying him with wonder and a bit of disbelief.

He'd miscalculated. A woman with Jade's experience would be suspicious if he put up too much resistance, particularly when she had to have, um... *felt* how interested he was in her.

Trying to steel himself against reacting, he moved close again. The key was to win her trust until he could find out what she'd done with the painting. Hopefully without losing either his pants or his mind in the process.

"Sorry," he whispered, reaching over to run his fingertips over her jaw, then across her full, bottom lip. She quivered beneath his hand, and he felt an answering flush of heat.

"I wanted to make sure you weren't falling into something you didn't want. The moonlight, the wine..."

She stared at him intently, as if gauging the truth of his words. Then she slowly nodded. "Maybe you're right. We can talk about the weather for a little while. You should see how things will heat up next month. July's nothing compared to August."

Sounded like she expected him to be around a while. But he planned to be long gone as soon as he retrieved his family's property.

"How'd you know your way around back here?" he asked as he shifted to focus on the stone angels instead of the fantasy woman who'd just been in his arms.

She didn't reply for a moment, merely watching with a measured glance. It was as if she was testing his resolve, wondering if he was really pulling away, or merely building the tension through verbal small talk.

Neither. He was merely trying to hold on to his sanity before he did something insane like haul up her dress to see whether she was wearing anything underneath.

From what he already knew about Jade Maguire, he suspected not.

Jade finally answered. "I'm pretty familiar with the city. Especially the historic buildings...like this one."

He knew a lot about her—her tour company—but wanted to see how much she'd reveal about herself. "You're a native?"

She nodded. "Born and raised. As were my parents, grandparents, great-grandparents and so on."

That surprised him. "You can really trace your genealogy back so far?"

She nodded. "Right back to the plantation."

The detective hadn't mentioned anything about that. "You're descended from some local plantation? From a long line of Southern belles?"

She laughed, but her laughter sounded more forced than amused. Shrugging, Jade rose from the bench, walked around toward the stone wall and leaned against it. She continued to sip her wine slowly. Then, seeming almost unaware she was doing so, she casually lifted one foot, slipping off one shoe, then the other. She arched a foot, stretching her leg, then her whole body, as sinuously as a cat. "Mmm, that feels wonderful."

Damn, even her feet were sexy. High-arched, delicate, with hot-pink-tinted nails. His mouth went dry as he pictured running his hands from those delicate ankles all the way up her legs. Up. Up. Under that black dress to find all her mysteries laid bare, waiting for him.

He closed his eyes as he drew in another deep breath

of hot night air. When he opened them, he found Jade watching him, a matching look of intensity on her face.

So, he wasn't the only one feeling it. This strange, instant attraction had affected them both.

If only he didn't have to hate her.

Trying to find something to distract himself with, he glanced at her wickedly high-heeled black shoes lying on the patio. He didn't understand how on earth women could contort their feet into such unnatural shapes. "Why do women wear the things if they're so painful? Do you really care what men think of your shoes?"

Shoes. A perfect topic of conversation for any woman. That heated look left her eyes as she gave him a pitying look. "No, of course we don't care what men think of our shoes. We care what *women* think of our shoes because we *all* love them."

She was right, though he still didn't get it. His own mother and sister felt the same way, as had every woman he'd ever dated. "All a man needs are two pairs of dress shoes, brown and black. Plus a casual brown pair for jeans, and some athletic shoes for sports."

Jade's shudder was almost comical. "You don't strike me as the type of man who has only four pairs of shoes in his closet."

"Ah, you can add," he said, not admitting she was right. "Most of the women I've met here tonight didn't look like they'd be able to."

This time, her surprised laughter sounded real, not forced. He found himself entranced by it, by the way her eyes lit up and crinkled a bit in the corners when she was really amused. She didn't look calculating now. Didn't look the seductress. Merely like an attractive, normal twenty-six-year-old. One who, under normal circumstances, he'd have been trying to get naked by now.

Naked. Bad thought. He swallowed hard, forcing it away.

"Oh, suh," she said, mimicking a thick accent, "I'm so awful lucky you don't have more shoes than I have little ole fingers," she retorted.

"Good thing," he said, getting up and moving to her side. He leaned his shoulder against the wall, turned sideways so he faced her. "Now tell me about your family's grand and glorious past on the plantation. Did your ancestors raise tobacco or cotton?"

"Cotton. And they *picked* it as much as raised it."

Good humor still kept her lips wide as he thought about her comment and finally understood it. "Really?"

She nodded. "We came from the wrong side of the Lancaster family tree. Via the mulatto mistress of the grand and valiant General Lester Lancaster, my great-great-great-great-grandfather." Then she added, "My great-great-great-great-grandmother, on the other hand, was a field hand who came to the attention of lecherous old Lester."

Descended of slaves. Fascinating. "I'm amazed you can track your family back so far."

"Many of the true locals can. That's why I know so much about the city—every bit of history, every piece of land." Her voice dropped, growing thick with intensity. This was a subject she truly cared about. "The architecture, the artifacts, the people, places and events. I've studied it all, read about it, been enthralled by it for as long as I can remember, examining it from both sides of my life to try to understand where I came from."

She seemed passionate about the subject. It sounded like he'd found the woman's real weakness. Beyond money, beyond sex or stealing, she was enthralled by the past. "Are you a historian?"

A mysterious smile widened her lips as she shook her head and returned to her seat, patting the bench until he sat down, too. Close to her. Very close. "Not exactly. But I do…dabble."

Dabble. He swallowed hard, wondering what other things the woman liked to *dabble* in. Naughty things?

"I like to explore things that interest me."

The way she said the word interest, combined with a slow lick of her lips and the way she watched him, sent his blood roaring through his veins.

He turned slightly so their faces were only a few inches apart. As were their bodies. "Things that interest you. You like to *study* them?"

She nodded, her gaze never straying from his face. "I like to study. And to touch." Her voice grew breathier. "To feel and to savor."

The heat was back, instant and unrelenting. He'd fought it valiantly for the half hour they'd been outside, but it surged back inside him. Every one of his senses was on alert, reacting to her nearness. Unbidden, his body moved closer. Closer. Close enough so they were sharing breaths and warmth and a physical desire that hung between them like a curtain.

"What about taste? Do you explore with your mouth?" He lifted his finger and brushed it across her full lower lip, tracing the soft skin in an intimate caress.

She licked at his skin, then bit the tip of his finger with her sharp white teeth. The contact was as exciting as it was unexpected. Jade was a little wild. He'd known that before they met. Now that wildness appeared to be driving her right back into his arms. And he didn't know if he'd be strong enough to step away this time.

"We done talking about the weather?" she asked, her whisper not taunting, not too assured, but full of a kind of hunger he hadn't heard in her voice before.

As if she, too, had recognized that, whatever had brought them both out here before, now there was nothing but pure, physical attraction.

He was as completely unable to resist it as any drowning man could resist grabbing on to a life ring. He needed her. To keep breathing. To keep surviving. To keep *living*.

So he took what she offered. He pulled her close, held her tight and lost himself in another deep kiss.

Whatever happened was going to happen, there was no escaping it anymore. Logic and tight control had evaporated under a mindless want and wild excitement he'd never experienced with anyone before.

He should be furious…with *himself*. But he had to acknowledge the truth. He planned to enjoy every blasted moment of it.

5

NOW, JADE. NOW.

It was time to act, to go ahead with her plan. If she didn't act now, she might lose all sense of purpose and forget that this wasn't a real seduction, a real interlude in a secret garden.

Besides, it was nearing midnight. Not pumpkin time. But toasting time. "Do you like to play sweet, wicked games, Ryan?" she asked when they drew apart for air.

He pressed his mouth to her neck, nibbling her pulse point. "Games? Fantasy games?"

She couldn't hold back a moan as his kiss grew hotter, deeper, and her mind filled with a dark fantasy of seductive vampires in shadowy Southern gardens.

"Yes," she finally replied, shifting on the bench so they were face-to-face. Her legs splayed, and the tight dress pushed higher up her thighs. She lifted them over his legs and slid closer, driving them both to the brink of pure sexual surrender.

"Wicked, naughty games. Fantasies. I've been having them ever since I saw you inside."

True. He just didn't have to know some of those fantasies included him being strung up by his private parts.

Speaking of private parts...his were definitely rising

to the occasion. She felt his heat, his thickness, against her leg, and nearly shuddered. Her revenge plan did not include actually getting to sample that impressive bulge of his in any way.

More's the pity.

"Tell me your fantasy, Jade. Are you a Southern belle stealing away to meet a forbidden lover?"

His whisper was husky, telling her he was just as affected by what was happening as she.

"Do you want me to be a dark stranger you stumble across in the dark? That isn't very far from the truth."

"No." *A vampire, a vampire,* she mentally answered, but she couldn't let the words escape her lips. Vampires weren't known to get naked in the moonlight.

"Tell me," he ordered. He lifted his mouth and brushed his lips against hers. She understood his tactic. He was taunting her, withholding more of those delightful kisses, nips and tastes until she admitted what she was thinking.

Good thing she'd thought this out in advance or she'd admit what she was really thinking—pulling her dress high enough to reveal her nakedness underneath, then unzipping his clothes and rubbing against all his hot skin until she came right on his lap. Then taking him for the ride of his life.

Not the plan, Jade. He's the one who's got to get caught and humiliated, not both of you.

Damn.

"You'll make my fantasy come true?"

He nodded, nipping at her lips, rubbing the tips of his fingers delicately along the neckline of her dress.

The contact electrified her and shot the tension up another notch. "I picture you naked in the moonlight."

"Not much of a fantasy," he replied as his fingers dipped lower, making incredible contact with her breast, but pulling away so quickly it nearly pained her instead of pleasuring her.

"There's more," she whispered, as they kissed again and again and she lowered her hand down his body.

She toyed with the buttons of his dress shirt, slipping them out, one by one. When she reached the waistband of his pants, she undid his belt and tugged the shirt free.

"Oh, God," he whispered as she ran her hand up his naked stomach and dug into those impossibly broad shoulders.

Focus. Focus, Jade, she told herself as he began to work the same magic. His hands were expert, smoothing here, pressing harder there, until he had her ready to go out of her mind with the need for a more intimate touch. He finally kissed her deeply again as he tugged the strap of her dress down and moved his hand to her breast.

She couldn't prevent a tiny cry from escaping her lips. "Oh, Ryan…"

He pulled away to look at her, then lowered his mouth to her breast. The touch of his fingers on her nipple had her writhing.

If this was going to happen, it had to happen immediately, or she was going to lose her resolve and have wild sex with a stranger in Mamie Brandywine's garden.

"Strip for me," she whispered.

He raised his head and looked at her, a half smile on his lips. "What?"

She looked at his body, not feigning a pure feminine appreciation for the long ridges of muscle and perfectly toned skin. "I want to watch you take off your clothes. I want you to reveal every inch of your body to me, with no touching. The anticipation is going to drive me out of my mind."

He began to laugh and tried to kiss her again. She put her hands over his lips. "I mean it, Ryan. I have this…this visual thing. I have extraordinary night vision and all my life I've been a creature of the night. I need to fill my eyes with you."

And she did. She longed to. Especially knowing that's all she could ever have.

"Because then when I fill my body with you," she continued, letting him hear her shaking arousal, "the pleasure will be so intense I don't know if I'll survive it."

He didn't respond for a moment. Then, without another word, he stood up and backed away from the bench. She wondered if she'd pushed too far, overplayed her hand.

When he dropped his white dress shirt off his shoulders, she knew she hadn't.

"Oh, my goodness," she whispered, not faking the response to seeing his thick arms, impossibly broad shoulders and hard, massive chest. "You hid so much beneath your suit."

He smiled. "You hide a lot behind your brown eyes."

"So we're even," she said on a breath, waiting for him to continue.

He reached for his waistband. But, heaven help her, Jade wasn't ready for that. She didn't know if she'd be able to withstand full-frontal without jumping on the man. Or at least tasting him a bit.

She shook her head, thrusting the sensual image from her mind, and pointed to his feet. His answering laugh said he knew what she wanted. "Anticipation, right?"

She nodded.

He took off his shoes and his socks, standing in bare feet and trousers just inches away, right in front of the gurgling fountain.

Reaching for his waist, he paused before unzipping. "Fair's fair, though. I don't think I got much of a glimpse of you."

She'd expected this. Giving him a mysterious smile, she reached for the other strap of her dress and pushed it down. Then, around her back, undoing the zipper just low enough to make the dress loosen across her breasts.

But before she let the black fabric drop away, she whispered, "I like to see, but I'm a little shy about being seen."

A snort of disbelief was his only answer.

"All right," she admitted. "Not shy...I like being mysterious." She showed him what she meant by drawing her red scarf around her shoulders and letting the two ends drape down her front. Then, and only then, did she allow the front of her dress to drop.

He watched, his expression hungry, as she moved the silky scarf across her taut nipples, almost cooing at the sensation.

"You're right," he whispered, wonder and surprise in his voice. "Anticipation is a wonderful thing."

She didn't know whether to be glad or disappointed that he hadn't insisted she remove the scarf. A big part of her—actually, two smaller, incredibly *sensitive* parts of her—were dying for his full attention. His eyes, his hands, his mouth. She wanted them all on her breasts.

Not in the plan.

"Now, Ryan?" she asked, not having to fake her sudden frenzy. She had to get this over with. It was nearly midnight. She could already see shadows of people moving into the solarium, where they'd gather to fill their champagne glasses for the toast.

He reached for his pants. Unzipped. Pushed them down. Jade watched through half-lowered lashes, not sure whether to be relieved or disappointed that he was wearing boxers underneath. Then it was time to move. She couldn't wait here, couldn't possibly watch him go one more step…couldn't get an eyeful of what she was leaving behind.

This was close enough.

She rose to her feet and approached him, still running the scarf across her nipples, keeping his attention firmly focused there.

"You done anticipating?" he asked.

"I have to touch you."

And she did. She stroked his shoulders, his stomach, all the while pushing him back, closer to the fountain. "Do you feel the spray against you?"

He nodded, leaning down to nip her neck, trying to nudge the scarf away from her breasts.

"It's so cool, isn't it?" she whispered. "Feels good against your hot skin."

Then she stopped speaking and simply let her body take over. She pressed against him, rubbing the silk between them with perfectly delicious friction. His groan told her how much he liked it.

It was so easy to rise on tiptoe, using a stone step below the fountain to bring her breasts closer to his mouth. She drew the scarf away slowly, inch by inch. Sliding it up over his head, she had it behind his back within a brief moment.

He didn't even notice. He was completely focused on her bared breasts. Focused on licking them, tasting them, drawing a nipple into his mouth with a suction so strong, so pleasurable it almost pained her.

"Just your mouth," she ordered when he tried to move his hands up to cup her.

He laughed against her chest, letting her capture his hands in her own, the scarf still sliding behind him.

Right around the back of one of the fountain cherubs. Through a loop over its wing. Then two quick twists around Ryan's hands and she was done.

"Jade?" He sounded only slightly alarmed.

"Don't you love this? Doesn't the silk feel amazing?" she replied, a little lost herself as he continued to lick her breasts.

Then she saw the lawn grow brighter, illuminated with the first of the floodlights, and knew it was time.

"Jade, I think someone's coming outside."

She didn't answer. She couldn't answer, she was suddenly so torn over what she was doing.

She wanted him, wanted him so badly. And what she was about to do would put him forever out of her reach.

Amazing sex with a fabulous stranger.

Or avenging her little sister.

As always in her life, family—loyalty to the other Dupré women—won out.

Without another word, she pulled away, bent down and yanked at his boxers. She had to pull them away from his body to get them over the massive erection, but Jade wasn't a strong enough woman to look. She kept her eyes firmly shut until the cotton hit the ground. Then she pulled up her dress.

And ran.

HE WAS GOING TO KILL her. Wrap his hands around her pretty pale throat and wring her conniving neck.

Ryan had never been so completely…*bested* by anyone.

Thankfully, her scheme to embarrass the hell out of him hadn't been a complete success. Yes, he'd been caught naked and alone, aroused, exposed and tied to a frigging statue.

But he hadn't been spotted by the entire crowd, as Jade had obviously hoped.

No, thankfully the only people who'd gotten the full view of him were Mamie Brandywine, owner of the inn, and Tally Jackson. The two women had stood framed in the doorway of the house, staring at him from across the yard. Their mouths had dropped.

So had their eyes. Down—straight down.

"Shit." The thought still made him cringe hours later in his bed.

Luckily, the two women had immediately backed into the house, telling the crowd some nonsense story about a sudden burst of rain falling on the lawn. So Ryan had had time to work free of the red scarf and pull on his clothes while cloaked in the shadows of the huge trees nearby.

Then he'd gone looking for Jade, slipping out of the garden through the back gate she'd used. But she'd disappeared like…a thief in the night.

Lying in his room late that night, he realized that, as furious as he was, he also had to hand it to her. She was good at what she did. Even if what she did was lie and cheat and steal and seduce.

Seduce. God in heaven, she really had. He'd gone down to that garden prepared to make her trust him, to reveal her secrets, so he could get some insight as to what she might have done with the painting.

Instead she'd kissed him. She'd invited him to touch

her. Her smell and the night air and the wind in the trees had successfully robbed him of all logic and made him give in to the most sensuous desire he'd ever felt. *Still* felt.

"Damn," he muttered in the darkness. He still wanted her, was rock hard again just thinking about how close they'd come.

"How close *you* came, moron. She was *a*cting the entire time."

But even as he whispered the words, he wondered if they were true. Jade might have set him up for a fall, then walked away—shoeless—laughing when he fell. But he'd guaran-damn-tee her legs had been wobbling a little bit during that walk.

He dangled one of her strappy, spike-heeled sandals—which he'd found on the patio where she'd left them—from the tip of his finger. "Cinderella you're not. And I'm sure as hell no Prince Charming."

She probably didn't realize he knew all about her—her full name, where she lived, how to find her, and how to get revenge. He didn't need a shoe to track down the girl who'd run away at midnight.

He'd give her her shoes back. No question about it. While he was at it, he'd force her to admit the truth. "She wanted me," he whispered aloud, certain he was right.

She had wanted more. She'd been just as lost as he had for a few minutes. Lost in that strange, powerful reaction they'd created in one another. If the light in the window hadn't come on...if there hadn't been a threat of exposure...if she'd been thinking only with the lower part of her body—as he had been—they might both have been caught in her spider web.

A knock sounded on his door, soft, tentative. "Now what?" he muttered.

"Mr. Stoddard? Would you like some company? Someone to talk things over with? May I come in for a little while?"

Good lord, his landlady. Ever since he'd returned to the house tonight, going in through a back kitchen door to avoid seeing anyone, she'd been tracking him. The look in her eyes when she'd seen him naked and hard was going to give him nightmares.

Good thing he'd locked the door. And put a chair under the knob, just in case the owner of the house decided to try testing her luck with a master key.

She knocked once or twice more. He remained silent, not wanting to have to change inns in the middle of the night.

Finally her footsteps moved away and he breathed a deep sigh of relief. He'd leave early tomorrow morning. No way was he going to stay here and risk getting attacked by an overly amorous old married lady who'd seen what he had to offer and wanted to take a closer look.

"I'll get you for this, Jade Maguire," he whispered softly so the inn owner wouldn't hear.

He'd come here to retrieve his grandmother's stolen property. That had been serious enough. Now things had gotten *really* personal. This battle had turned downright intimate.

Jade might have won the first skirmish. She might even have seen his…*weapon.*

But he had not yet begun to fight.

JADE NOTICED THE obnoxious tourist immediately upon meeting her tour group at the cemetery the following night. She couldn't stand the type. Loud, inconsiderate, not caring about the history of the area he was about to visit, but only wanting to act manly and disbelieving of the haunted stories he'd paid to hear.

She knew what he was thinking. His whole demeanor demanded, "Scare me or I'll want my money back." She'd met his kind before and, on every occasion, they'd nearly ruined an otherwise successful tour.

"I'm going to kill Freddy for this," she told Daisy, her employee, the guide who'd just completed the early evening ghost tour of Savannah.

"I think this is the fifth time he's called in sick this month," Daisy said, sounding disgusted. "You know I'd take it if I could."

Jade looked at her best worker and good friend. "I know you would. I'm sorry, I'm not blaming you. I know how you've been looking forward to your boyfriend coming home."

Jade didn't add the next words that crossed her mind—from jail. But Daisy probably knew she'd thought them.

The young girl was a doll. Supportive, hard-working. Much too good for the car-stealing jerk she loved.

So what if Daisy was a goth, transplanted from New Orleans, who was still into the Louisiana vampire culture? The black clothes, black spiked hair, black nails and black circles around her eyes worked well for the night tours. That's why Daisy had become the most popular guide Jade employed. Worth every penny it had taken Jade to lure her away from her second cousin, who ran a similar company down in New Orleans.

Freddy, on the other hand, wasn't worth the trouble it was going to take to fire him. She'd already started looking for someone else, not only because Freddy wasn't dependable. He also had a nasty habit of hitting on the unattached women in his tour groups.

"Are we going on this thing or what?" the loud man in the back asked.

Jade smothered a sigh. She'd known he'd be trouble when she saw his long shorts, coupled with shin-high white socks with the requisite red stripe around the elastic top. She hadn't even needed to see the brightly-flowered Hawaiian shirt, camera slung around his neck, big ugly glasses and ball cap to know he had "difficult" and "tasteless" written all over him.

"We'll be departing in a few minutes," Jade told the audience, implicitly telling the man to be patient.

The crowd was a big one tonight. Mostly college-age kids and young adults. The families typically came to the early tour, not this one, which wouldn't end until ten-thirty, at the Winter Garden inn.

Pushy tourists, however, seemed to show up at every single one. Lucky her.

"We gonna actually see any ghosts on this tour? Or just hear made-up stories about them?"

Jade shot the gum-chewing loudmouth a look that told him to shut up. He merely smirked, his long mustache covering his top lip so that he looked like a walrus.

"Don't give the city any more ghosts tonight," Daisy said, sounding amused. "We have enough murder victims for the tour. And I can't afford to be out of work because my boss is doing ten to twenty for justifiable homicide."

"Justifiable being the key," she replied, giving Daisy a wry look.

Daisy grinned, the happy look somewhat incongruous given her blood-red lips and paste-white skin, but the goodness shone through. Daisy was the first to admit she wasn't a vampire wannabe, merely a player.

She liked the look, but nothing else that went with it. That was one of the reasons she'd left New Orleans, which sometimes took its "playing" a little too seriously.

Jade was so glad she had. She valued Daisy's friendship, and squeezed her hand to let her know it. "If things don't go well tonight…"

"They will," Daisy said, not letting anything spoil her vision of her reunion with her ex-con boyfriend.

"I mean *if* they don't…then come by, okay? I'm sure I'll be up late."

Daisy smirked. "If I thought you'd be up late for the right reason—because you actually had a man in your bed, instead of a juicy book and a vibrator—I wouldn't come anywhere near your place."

Rolling her eyes, Jade didn't admit that Daisy's description was probably closer to the truth than anyone would realize. Except for the vibrator part. She wouldn't dare such a thing with Auntie Lula Mae staying with her. The old woman had ears like a hawk and would demand to know what the buzzing sound was. And once she'd seen the cute little toy—which Jade had bought off an Internet site when she'd hit fifteen months straight without sex—she'd probably want to know how to get one of her own.

Eeew.

But once Lula Mae returned home to Mama's house…well, Jade predicted her vibrating friend would get a good workout. She certainly could have used it after her incredible interlude with Ryan Stoddard the night before.

She still shook, remembering the intensity of feeling—of pleasure—they'd shared in the Medford garden. If the light hadn't come on, she might very well have been the one caught bare-ass naked by the fountain. Because she'd wanted nothing more at that moment other than him. Nothing. But. Him.

"Have fun," Daisy said as she walked off down the street.

Jade grimaced, waved goodbye, and led the group past the cemetery. She'd have to keep a smile on her face and ignore the troublemakers on the tour. As well as put any and all evil, distracting thoughts of sex out of her mind. This was her livelihood, after all.

There was one surefire way to make sure she kept a smile on her face. All she had to do was think about Ryan Stoddard, tied up, naked and discovered by fifty or so tuxedoed millionaires.

Naked. Humiliated. Embarrassed. Paid back. Unfulfilled.

Okay, that wasn't so satisfying, since they'd *both* been unfulfilled. Anyway, somehow, *naked* and *Ryan Stoddard* were three words she shouldn't have put in the same sentence.

God, he'd been glorious. Impossibly big and hard and toned and perfect. Covered with smooth skin that still made her fingers itch to touch, nearly twenty-four hours later.

Walking away had been about punishing him. But it had punished her as well. She'd never been as physically aroused by a man as she had in those moments before she'd remembered she was out for revenge. Not orgasms.

Though, those would have been pretty nice, too.

No, not from him. Vibrators were just as efficient, and they didn't go around seducing twenty-one-year-olds.

Or, if they did, at least they could be put back in a drawer.

"Next week. A woman can survive one week without a man or a vibrator," she told herself.

Though, to be honest, she found herself wishing Aunt Lula Mae were a little more hard of hearing, as were most people her age.

"Where's the ghosts?" she heard from a dozen people back.

Mr. Obnoxious.

Pasting a smile on her face, she thrust the incredible memory of Ryan Stoddard's body and face and hands and mouth out of her mind. He was out of her life. Probably out of Savannah after the embarrassment he'd suffered the night before. She'd never see him again, and he'd think twice about the women he went after.

All's well that ends well.

But that still didn't dispel the hint of emptiness inside her when she imagined what might have been.

6

SHE HADN'T RECOGNIZED him. She'd noticed him—oh, he'd made absolutely sure she'd notice him. If he'd tried to blend in and be unobtrusive, she'd probably have paid more attention. Deceptive people were sneaky and untrusting that way.

So Ryan had gone out of his way to be as obvious as possible.

If any of his buddies, clients or former girlfriends could see him now—dressed like one of those old farts who cruised the mall, looking for high school girls in tight shorts to drool over...

It was a perfect disguise.

Ryan had even begun to enjoy the tour once he'd let down his guard a bit. Jade stayed far away from him after his one attempt to move up front. He'd almost laughed when he'd sidled up behind her. He'd been right under her nose, hidden behind some saggy, hideously ugly clothes, a ball cap, thick eyeglasses complete with ugly black rims and a fake mustache.

She'd never even realized. She'd moved away, putting several people between them, and hadn't paid him a bit of attention since.

He had to hand it to her—she wasn't bad at her job. She had a natural theatrical flare, not surprising since she'd proven herself such a consummate actress last night.

But there was more than performance. She seemed passionate about her work. She answered questions about the history and architecture of the area without a moment's hesitation.

So she knew her stuff. Big deal. Any thief would have to have a good memory. The better to maneuver through dark houses. Or dark gardens.

"And here," she was saying somewhere ahead of him, "is the famous bar where an infamous pirate is rumored to demand his rum, even to this day."

A drink. That sounded good. If only to steel himself for what he was about to do to this woman very, very soon.

Last night she'd been the one who'd had the upper hand, and he'd ended up naked and restrained. Tonight, it was her turn.

By the end of the tour, when they reached the Winter Garden House, Ryan had made sure to be as much of a pest as he could. He was definitely the most noticeable one on the tour.

So she'd definitely notice when he disappeared.

He wondered why Jade included the house on the tour, considering it was owned by the wealthy side of her family. According to the tour, the place had been on that side of the family for decades. Did Jade come here night after night to look at what her side had been denied? Perhaps to see the kinds of things—paintings, jewelry, antiques—that she'd coveted but never had as a child?

Damn, he really needed to stop this psychoanalyzing stuff. It was stupid and he was no expert. He knew next to nothing about the woman, so why he'd started pegging her as a poor relation out to right the wrongs done to her ancestors, he had no idea.

Maybe because he didn't want her to be just an average, avaricious thief. Maybe because he wanted to *allow* himself to like her.

Or at least to get involved with her.

"Stupid, stupid," he muttered to himself as the tour finished up. Henry, Jade's uncle, had greeted them briefly, then disappeared somewhere inside the depths of the house. A uniformed waitress supplied everyone on the tour with a complimentary cognac or champagne as Jade wrapped up her story about the ghost who haunted the attic of the building.

Time to act. Now, while the guests tipped her, thanked her, and exited to the street. She was still in the parlor, and a cluster of people were moving through the foyer to the door.

He made his move. "I want to look at the upstairs rooms," he grumbled aloud, scratching his belly and being as disgusting as possible.

His words earned him a look of disdain from one of the women on the tour.

"Paid a lot of money, I should get to see upstairs!" He said the words loudly enough to be overheard, then sauntered away.

From behind him, he heard a buzz of conversation. Ryan merely strolled down the hall as if he owned the place. And up the stairs he went.

It would take about thirty seconds for one of the other customers to rat him out to Jade. Sixty more to usher everyone else out of the house. She'd be looking for him immediately thereafter.

Lucky for him this was a weeknight and the inn was relatively empty. Only two other upstairs rooms were occupied and both had their doors firmly shut. After darting into his own room, he turned on a light, sat in one of the antique frou-frou chairs…and waited.

"Sir. Sir, you can't be up here!"

A minute and a half. Damn, she was quick.

"Huh?" he asked, rising to his feet as Jade rushed into the room, her fists clenched, her face red.

"You cannot come upstairs to the private rooms. Mr. Porter allows us to visit the downstairs rooms only. You need to leave immediately."

Keeping his cap down in case the mustache and big, ugly glasses weren't a good enough disguise, he lifted his camera. Continuing to mimic the guy with the thick Bronx accent who'd done some repair work for him last month, he said, "I just wanted to get some pictures of this here old bed. People musta been sleepin' awful cozy in the old days." Then he cackled. "And I bet it squeaked when the getting got good."

She sighed heavily, looking disgusted. Ryan didn't know whether to be delighted with his own perfor-mance, or offended that she really thought he was some tasteless, tacky tourist.

"I must insist that you come with me right now."

She stepped closer. Closer. One step more. Until he *had* her.

Quick as he could, he moved behind her and shut the door. The old-fashioned lock worked—he'd tested it earlier. It was easy enough to twist the lock and drop the key into his pocket.

"What do you think you're doing?" Jade asked, looking more outraged than afraid.

He didn't answer. Instead he reached for the long strap of his camera and carefully lifted it over his head, not removing the cap.

"Unlock the door right now, or I'll call for help."

"Will you?" he asked, no longer trying to hide his real voice.

He reached for the top button of the hideous Hawaiian shirt and began to undo it. Jade's eyes widened as she began to realize the kind of trouble she could be in.

He was tempted to let her be afraid, but something inside him resisted. He wanted her afraid of *him*. Of his retribution. But not that some whacked out stranger was about to rape her.

"I know karate and I have a wicked herpes out-break," she said, her voice thready. She curled her fingers into fists at her sides, obviously prepared to fight him in spite of her fear.

Ryan couldn't help laughing as he finally lifted the ball cap from his head and pulled the glasses from his face. "Well, then, I guess I should count myself lucky you stopped things where you did last night."

Then she got it. Her jaw dropped and she stepped back, wrapping her fingers in the velvety antique curtains behind her.

"Ryan…"

He peeled off the mustache, wincing a little as the spirit gum stuck to his lip. "Hello, Jade."

"How did you find me?" she asked, her voice breathy. She looked more nervous now than when she'd feared he was a rapist.

He didn't answer at first, merely letting the tension build as he unfastened another button. Then another. She never took her eyes off him and he'd swear her breathing picked up its pace as more and more of his body was revealed.

He'd been right—she hadn't faked her responses

last night. She'd wanted him. Badly. Which would definitely work to his advantage now.

"Did you really think you were going to be so hard to track down?" He could hear the tightly controlled anger in his own voice as the memory of what had happened between them last night returned full-force.

He'd been totally focused on what she'd done, leaving him there naked and humiliated. Now he was remembering more. How she'd felt in his arms. How her lips had tasted. The way her hands had touched him.

He didn't know whether to tear her clothes off and finish what they'd started or lock her in the closet for tormenting him.

"I, uh, figured you'd leave the city this morning. As soon as you were able."

He stepped closer. She stepped back. "You figured wrong. And by the way, your scheme didn't exactly work."

For the first time, she looked less nervous and more surprised. "It didn't?"

Shaking his head, he quirked a half smile, full of condescension, not amusement. "Your friend Tally spotted me. She made sure the guests didn't come out for their toast."

He didn't tell her about the amorous old innkeeper spying him, too. That would have given her too much satisfaction.

"So, all's well that ends well," she said with a nervous laugh, and he sensed the irony in her words. She tried to step around him. "Just a little joke and no harm done, right?"

He moved yet again, blocking her way with his body. After undoing the last button of the hideous shirt, he pushed it from his shoulders.

"Wh-what are you doing?" she asked. The lick of her lips and the shake in her voice indicated where her thoughts had gone.

To him. Undressing. In a bedroom. One night after they'd been so incredibly intimate in so many ways.

"Do you know how unpleasant it was to wear this disguise?" he asked. "I had to buy this shirt at a used clothing store."

The shirt dropped to the floor. Her eyes dropped to his chest, his stomach.

When he reached for the fastening of the ugly old-man shorts, her eyes dropped again. "You can't…"

"Can't what? Can't take off the ridiculous disguise I had to wear in order to get you alone again?"

Her stare never wavered as he unbuttoned the shorts, unzipped the zipper, and dropped them to the floor.

"Oh, my God," she whispered, reaching up to clutch her throat.

"Nothing you haven't seen before, is it, Jade? Though, you didn't stick around long enough to really see how you affected me last night."

She could see now, though. Her whole face was flushed, her lips parted and wet as she stared at him. All of him, including the erection he wasn't trying to hide.

He'd always assumed he was a normally built man. But the shocked hunger in her eyes told him he'd caught her off guard.

"No, you're right. I d-didn't see you that well," she stammered.

He kicked off the ugly shoes, then bent to peel off the socks. Then he rose, standing in front of her completely naked. Uncaring, not bothering even to pretend to be self-conscious.

She looked like she wanted to run. She looked like she wanted to jump on him. She looked like she needed someone to tell her what to do.

So he did.

"Take off your dress and get into the bed, Jade."

Noooo, no, this couldn't be happening. Not to her. Not here. Not with *him*.

But it was. She was so hungry, so full of want for this man that she couldn't think, couldn't move, couldn't breathe.

He'd just ordered her to strip and get into bed. Jade didn't take orders from anybody. And yet she wanted to do as he said more than she'd ever wanted anything.

She wanted *him*. All of him. His mouth, those incredibly thick arms. The flat washboard stomach, rippled with muscles, slimming down into a pair of lean male hips. And, oh mercy, *lower*. He was thick and hard and throbbing and he hadn't so much as touched her.

Lucky thing she hadn't looked carefully last night before she'd mustered up her last bit of willpower and escaped through the back gate. Because if she'd seen what she was giving up, she might never have left.

For one moment, a shot of gladness swept through her that no other woman at the party last night had seen him either—other than Tally, who was notoriously vain about her looks and hadn't been wearing her glasses. So she couldn't have gotten too good a look.

Why she felt territorial over this man—a man she'd sworn she hated—she had no idea. But she did. She *did*.

"You can't force me," she whispered, trying to come up with some resolve.

"You owe me."

"I owe you sex?"

He shook his head. "Sex isn't the right word."

"An apology? Okay, I'm sorry."

"That's not it, either, though I'm glad to hear you say it."

He obviously hadn't heard the sarcasm in her voice.

"Even though I know you don't mean it."

Maybe he had.

"I mean, you owe me a chance."

A chance for…revenge? To punish her? Hurt her in some diabolical way as she'd hurt him? "To do what?"

He lifted his hand to her face and ran his fingers across her lips. She couldn't resist nipping at them. The frustration inside her required the outlet. It was incredibly tense to stand here fully clothed, with a fully aroused, powerful, gorgeous naked man.

"I mean," he continued softly, "you owe me a chance to convince you to stay this time."

That rocked her right in her shoes. But before she could respond, he curled his hand around her head, wrapping his fingers in her hair. Not giving her time to refuse, he pulled her close, capturing her mouth in a kiss full of heat and anger, desire and lust. His tongue swept over hers as he nearly drank from her, consuming every bit of energy she might otherwise have used to protest.

When he finally pulled away, he looked down at her with wide eyes. His lips were parted, his breathing ragged. And between him, the hard, living proof of his hunger grew even harder. Stronger. Until she couldn't help but reach down and encircle him with her hand.

He groaned, low and long, as she caressed him, stroking his length with her fingers, giving out a helpless little whimper of her own at the feel of all that satin skin around that rock-hard heat.

"Give me a chance to make you *unable* to walk away this time," he whispered hoarsely.

Jade could no more resist than she could have said no to a chance for eternal happiness. There was no thinking. No logic. No revenge, remorse or family loyalty.

Nothing but overpowering *want*.

Stepping back, she reached around and unfastened her long black skirt. It fell to her feet and she kicked it aside. Ryan's eyes devoured her as hers had done with him. She hadn't gotten this far undressed last night.

"Ahh...I never got to find out what you were wearing under your dress," he murmured as he reached for her hip. He toyed with the elastic strap of her silky black thong, tugging it away from her skin and caressing her with his fingertips. "Was it something like this?"

She shook her head, reaching up to tug her tight tank top up and over her head. "Actually," she said as she threw it to the floor, "it was nothing like this. I mean *nothing*."

He smiled, catching her meaning. "Somehow I knew you were bold enough to come to that party without any underwear."

She smiled back. Then the lightness faded away and he simply stared at her clad in her black sandals, the panties and a matching lacy black bra that pushed her breasts up in pure invitation.

"You're beautiful," he said, wrapping his arms around her waist and pulling her close. He nuzzled her chest, running his tongue over the curves of her breast. When he slipped lower, to tease one achingly sensitive nipple, she shuddered. Her legs felt weak, unable to support her, and she leaned into him.

"To bed, Jade," he said, sweeping her up into his arms and carrying her across the room.

"Please tell me you didn't just steal this room," she whispered before she was completely lost to sensation.

He chuckled. "I'm registered. It's my room."

"Thank heaven."

Then she gave herself over to it, to the insane frenzy she'd felt for this man since the moment she'd laid eyes on him.

He slowly stripped off her sandals and her panties, stroking her long legs, running his hand teasingly across her curls until she shivered.

"Please…"

"Absolutely."

He reached for the front clasp of her bra and undid it with two fingers, watching as it popped open. A deep groan told her how much he liked what he saw.

"Lie back," he ordered, nudging her over on the bed as he knelt beside her. She did, raising her arms above her head and writhing on the sheets, loving the coolness of them against her skin.

"Tell me you wanted me last night," he murmured against her breast. "That whatever the hell made you do it, it was just as painful for you to walk away as it was for me to see you leave."

She couldn't lie. Not now, when he was touching her like this. Not when he was absolutely right. "I wanted you," she admitted, her voice breaking as he lavished attention on one sensitive nipple with his mouth, and the other with his fingertips. "So much I sat in my car and shook for ten minutes afterward."

"Yeah? Well I stood in my shower and jacked off for ten minutes afterward."

She groaned, inflamed by the hot, exciting words,

just as she was inflamed by the amazing things his hands and mouth were doing to her.

She closed her eyes, savoring it all. Every sensation built upon the last one. His touch, his smell, the way his lips felt…there, oh, yes, there on her neck…and on her jaw. The way his strong, rough hands slid up each arm as he covered her. The clasp of their fingers.

And then…

"What are you doing?" she said when she felt the first chill of cold metal against her wrist.

Before she had her answer, the second one was equally enclosed.

"Handcuffs?" she said, realizing he'd restrained her. He'd handcuffed her to the bed.

Under other circumstances, she might have enjoyed something so naughty. But this was their first time. And he hadn't asked. He'd simply gone ahead with something that was usually reserved for a bit later in a relationship. Like at least past the first date!

"I'm not comfortable with this, Ryan," she said, looking him in the eye to convey her seriousness.

He met her stare intently, then pressed one quick kiss against her lips. "I'm sorry, babe," he said. "You don't have a choice.

She only began to understand when he rose from the bed and reached for a pair of jeans draped on a nearby chair.

No, he couldn't be doing this. Couldn't possibly have done this to her all for…

"Paybacks are hell, Jade."

She heard the regretful tone in his voice but chose to ignore it, focusing only on her rising fury. "Unfasten me right now, you bastard."

He shook his head, calmly pulling on a black T-shirt.

He watched her strain and twist against the cuffs. If he'd smirked, if he'd looked triumphant, she probably would have found the adrenaline to rip the frigging headboard apart. But he continued to look sorry so she tried to calm down. "Okay. I probably deserved this. I did something pretty wicked to you last night."

Not that he hadn't deserved it, too.

"Someday you'll have to tell me why you did it."

Over her dead body. So he could go off and torment Jenny with the same kind of revenge? Not a chance.

God, the thought of him with her younger sister made her sick. She couldn't believe she'd forgotten, in these few intensely erotic minutes, that she couldn't have him. She hated the idea of him sharing anything this intimate with Jenny. Hated imagining Jenny seeing him, being touched by him.

But probably *not* being handcuffed by him.

"I...I thought you were too cocky," she said, scrambling for something that sounded reasonable. "I was trying to bring you down a peg. Teach you not to be so overconfident with women."

He leveled a stare on her, thankfully keeping his attention focused on her face and not on her naked body so completely at his mercy. "And I suppose you've never heard of just telling a guy no?"

Okay, lame story and he wasn't buying it. "Look, you're right, it was awful and I regret it." She wiggled the handcuffs. "Really, *really* regret it. So let's call it even. Okay?"

He sat in the chair, pulling on some shoes. "Sorry. Too late." Without another word, he stood and walked over to her pile of clothes. "Just in case you somehow manage to make like Houdini..." He picked them up—skirt, top, sandals, undies and all—and headed toward the door.

"Dammit, Ryan, get back here! You can't do this to me." She couldn't imagine anything worse than being left here, exposed, naked, vulnerable.

He looked over his shoulder. "I think you need a lesson. Be thankful I'm not leaving the door open so you can be spotted by anyone happening along."

Okay, *that* would be worse.

When he reached for the knob, her hope plummeted, and she tried one last desperate trick. "Ryan," she said, keeping her voice low and seductive, "look, you made your point, just like I did last night. Are we going to let these silly little games get in the way of what we could have together?"

That got him. He froze, hand on knob, and turned to look at her. She stretched sinuously, knowing gravity and a flat surface were helping her body look its absolute best.

He devoured her with his stare. Pure sexual hunger shone on his face and she had to twist a little on the bed as sensations she'd thought he'd killed with the snap of a handcuff returned full-force.

She didn't know what she'd do if he changed his mind. Brain him, or welcome him. Push him off her or dive on top of him herself.

In any case, she felt sure she had succeeded in changing his mind. Right up until the minute he opened the door.

That killed the moment. "You son of a bitch, I'll scream. If you do this, you'd better come back armed, because I'm going to kill you when you unlock me."

His laugh was wicked and made her even more furious. "You won't scream because I don't think you want your uncle Henry finding you like this."

He was right. The fiend.

"And you won't kill me, Jade." He walked the few steps back to the bed. Then he bent down, sliding his hand around her head and capturing her mouth in another of those incredible hot, wet kisses that fed her desire even as it fueled her anger.

When he lifted his mouth, she couldn't say a word, could only stare at him in disbelief.

"Once you're sufficiently paid back for last night," he said, "maybe then we can finish what we started."

While she still panted, reacting from their kiss, trying to decide whether she was bloody furious or aroused enough not to care, he bent down and retrieved something from the floor. "Here. I won't leave you without any of your belongings."

She held out hope that he'd at least give her a shirt or something to cover up. When he dropped her black, spike-heeled shoes—the ones she'd forgotten in the garden the night before—she could only groan. And try to kick him.

He easily evaded her foot. Then he got up, walked to the door and left the room. Leaving her, the always put-together Jade Maguire, naked and handcuffed to his bed.

7

A MONK WOULDN'T HAVE BEEN able to walk out of that bedroom without regretting it the minute he'd shut the door. And Ryan was no damned monk.

"She's gonna be furious," he whispered, leaning against the door, knowing he'd be facing an enraged woman when he returned to the inn. Even more enraged by his parting shot and final kiss. A woman with pride as great as hers would *never* let him take up where they'd left off. She'd be stewing over it, getting herself good and worked up and ready to rip him apart the minute he walked back in the room.

No second chance. No forgiveness. Certainly no body-rocking sex, which he needed right now like a starving man needed food.

But only with her. How could he deal with that? The only woman he wanted—the only woman he literally hungered for—was doomed to hate his guts forever and ever, amen.

Maybe it was just as well. He would need her hatred, her anger, to keep his defenses up. He'd come here to Savannah to expose her as a thief. To retrieve his family's property.

Not to become her lover. Not to worship every inch of her body, starting with her curved foot and those endlessly long soft legs. Not to kiss the hollow of her stomach or sample again the dusky sweet nipples he could still taste on his tongue. Not to find her secrets buried behind the curly patch between her legs.

Not to discover why he was affected by her as he'd never been affected by any other woman in his whole life.

"Moron," he called himself, thrusting away from the door to stalk down the stairs, trying to shake off his lust with every pounding step. He was going to lose it in his pants if he let his mind go down that road again. Once he got back from his mission, freed her and was alone again, he'd take care of himself. His hand would be a poor substitute for any part of the body he'd left lying on his bed. But it would have to do.

Almost not realizing he was doing it, he lifted Jade's shirt to his face and breathed in her sweet, flowery scent. How twisted was that? He was a total idiot. He'd let a con woman make him start fantasizing about the kind of sexual relationship he'd never known. And maybe about even more.

No way could he ever like, respect and enjoy the company of someone he couldn't trust an inch. Yet those were the feelings he had with Jade whenever he let down his guard, let himself forget why he'd sought her out in the first place. It was easy to forget. Especially when she was in his arms.

Or naked.

Balling her clothes in his fist, he reached into the pocket of her skirt and found what he'd hoped to—a small key ring. He knew her address. The P.I. had given him that. But the keys were a lucky break. Now he wouldn't have to actually break anything while he did his nighttime breaking and entering.

Fifteen minutes later, he was parked on a small,

quiet tree-lined street in an older part of town. Formerly townhouses for the wealthy, the buildings all around had been converted into apartments or condos. Jade's building wasn't exactly shabby, but it had the same worn, run-down feel of the rest of the street. Not for the first time, he wondered about her motives for stealing.

"Maybe she really just needed the money," he mused aloud.

Coming from a wealthy family, and having a good job, he'd never been put in the position of needing money. He liked to think he'd never resort to stealing, but until he was actually tested, he didn't know what he'd do if, say, a loved one needed food, medicine or shelter. It was something to consider, anyway.

He got out of his car, closing the door quietly behind him. As he slipped through the shadows of overgrown trees and bushes, he again noted the condition of the building. The lawn was wild and unkempt, a tangled profusion of vines climbing up one entire wall. Pretty, but dingy-looking at the same time.

He wondered again about her finances. How much money could a tour guide operator make? How much did her family rely on her? The mother was the talk of the town—the poor relation to the wealthy cousin living in the Winter Garden House.

He began to see the possibilities. Perhaps Jade had gone on this stealing spree to support her unusual family, from the man-hopping mother to the self-absorbed actress sister in New York to the old voodoo priestess aunt. It sounded like her mother liked to live the good life. With Jade's father's job as a bartender, perhaps that lifestyle had come at too high a cost.

Now, with Jade's mother having married some guy

and gone off on a cruise, maybe Jade wouldn't be on the hook for everyone else. Supporting herself on a tour guide's salary shouldn't be difficult. Maybe she could give up her other, illegal life.

Like she'd give it up for *him?* A near-stranger? A man who'd left her naked and helpless in a hotel room?

Fat friggin' chance.

Still, the thought that Jade had done what she'd done to help her family made it slightly less awful to imagine. Maybe even more forgivable. And for some crazy reason, he found himself *wanting* to forgive her.

Entering Jade's ground-floor home as quietly as… well, a burglar, he found himself in a dark living room. He paused, letting his eyes adjust to the low light, provided by a single lamp lit deeper inside the apartment.

The hint of light cast enough of a glimmer to let him get a quick layout of the room. Sofas and loveseats, one would think. But not for Jade. She had a few groupings of uncomfortable-looking chairs, but the center of the room was dominated by, of all things, a fountain.

He groaned. Ryan never wanted to look at another fountain again as long as he lived. But he couldn't help giving it a second glance. Talk about your unusual room décor. This one looked like it should have been outside, in a garden. Or, considering the crying angels, maybe even in a graveyard.

The woman had issues.

Moving further into the apartment, he again noticed that, though clean and colorful, Jade's home didn't offer much in the way of standard comforts. He didn't see a television. No stereo. In the kitchen, he found only the basics, devoid of any fancy appliances—no dishwasher at all.

"So where do you stash the good stuff, Jade?" he whispered.

He turned to leave the kitchen, determined to find out, and was shocked to see two white eyes staring back at him from about five feet above the floor.

He blinked. Looked again. They were still there.

"I'm not seeing this."

The eyes spoke. "Don' min' me, Mr. Tief. No silver, no jewels, but don' take my word. You go ahead an' look around."

Holy shit. He knew without a doubt who was speaking to him. Not a ghost. This was the voodoo witch. The one Tally had been talking about at the party. "It's not what you think…"

"How you know what I tink?" Her voice held a rhythmic cadence and her words rolled off her tongue, hinting of island secrets and mysteries.

"I'm not a thief."

Hearing a click, he was caught off guard when she turned on the overhead light. The sharp illumination hurt his darkness-accustomed eyes, and he had to close them.

He was nervous about reopening them, wondering what he'd see. If he had to be discovered, he'd almost prefer to be caught by a gun-toting redneck than a witch.

Finally he steeled himself for anything—including shrunken heads or chicken claws around her neck—and opened his eyes.

She grinned.

So did he. He couldn't help it. She looked very, *very* normal. "Hi."

"Hi, Mr. Tief."

Her polished brown skin was much darker than

Jade's. He wasn't surprised by her race, given what he knew about Jade's family. Her face was smooth and nearly unlined. But her hair was a wiry mix of black and gray, with gray appearing to be the winner. Her smile was accentuated by the whitest, largest teeth he'd ever seen. And she wore an old-lady housecoat that fell to just above a pair of very knobby brown knees. On her feet were bunny slippers.

Okay, no one with bunny slippers on her feet was going to chant a few words and cause all his hair to fall out or make his nuts stop doing their job.

"You find anyt'ing good?" she asked, as matter-of-factly as she'd ask an invited guest.

He shook his head. "You don't understand. I'm not a thief."

"You come here to take something from us?"

"Well…"

"Den you a tief. A good-looking one, though."

"So why haven't you called the police?"

She shrugged. "You not a dangerous man. I can tell as soon as you come in the front door."

She was right, though he felt mildly insulted that he didn't have even the tiniest bit of danger written anywhere on his aura.

"How you get in?"

"I used Jade's key," he admitted.

That didn't seem to phase her, either. She simply nodded. "Where is she?"

He hesitated. If he could get the old woman to help him somehow, maybe he could end this thing tonight. But it probably wouldn't be easy if she found out what he'd done.

She crossed her skinny arms over her old-lady chest and gave him a sideways smile. "What you do with

Jade? And don' lie." She wagged her eyebrows. "I'll know if you lie."

"She's handcuffed to my bed at the Winter Garden House," he found himself saying. Then he groaned, wondering how the hell he'd let those words spill out of his mouth. Maybe she *had* hexed him because he'd had no intention of telling the truth.

The old woman's eyes widened and she let out a bark of laughter that made her whole body shake. The white smile became even whiter. She clutched a chair, almost snorting with laughter, then clapped a hand to her mouth. "Oh, no," she lisped, "there go my good teefs."

He didn't know what she meant until she spat out a full set of dentures into her hand, giving him a wide, gummy grin. He began to laugh with her.

"Din' have time to glue 'dem in right when I hear you comin' in to steal from us." Before he protested, she held up a hand, smooth and work-worn, but still strong and capable. "Don' worry. I know now who you are. You flash de folks at de fancy party last night."

Oh, God, so much for his hope that Tally Jackson and Mamie Brandywine hadn't told their tale. "You heard about that, hmm?"

She shrugged, not explaining. "So you getting even?"

He shrugged. "Sort of."

The old woman casually retrieved a glass, filled it with water and dropped her teeth into it with a little plop. Then she put a pot of water on the stove, retrieved two mugs and a container of tea leaves. "We talk over a drink."

And somehow, though he'd come here to steal what had been stolen, he found himself sitting in a quiet kitchen, drinking a cup of delicious and strangely spiced tea, with Lula Mae Dupré, voodoo priestess of Savannah.

JADE FUMED, CURSED and muttered for the first ten minutes after Ryan had walked out of the room, leaving her helpless on the bed.

Helpless. What an unbelievably awful feeling. Jade hadn't felt helpless, ever. Her mother's romantic life had been a nonstop adventure, but otherwise Jade had been the product of a normal home. Her family—both close and extended—was a secure one. She'd always felt loved, both before and after Daddy's death, and had been raised to believe she could be anyone, achieve absolutely anything.

Except make handcuffs magically open.

"You sneaky S.O.B.," she whispered, finally allowing a bit of reluctant admiration for her adversary to enter her mind. He'd gotten her, but good.

After last night, he had to have figured she had it coming. *She* knew why she'd abandoned him in the garden at the Medford place—because of Jenny. But he didn't know. He must have figured her for some game-playing sexual psycho who got her kicks leading men on, building them up—way, way up, in his case, she recalled with a gulp—then letting them crash and burn.

His retribution was pretty fair, considering he'd at least shut the door to the room. Nobody would be seeing her here, unlike where she'd left him last night.

"That still doesn't mean I'm not going to kill him," she muttered through tight teeth.

But for now, she focused only on covering herself. Bad enough to have to face the man when he got back,

knowing he'd won this round. She didn't want to have
to do it while stark naked, laid bare for his perusal.

Or his *pursual.*

She couldn't handle that. Couldn't even think of him
coming back into the room and doing what he'd threat-
ened—counting the score even and trying to finish
what they'd started.

She dreaded that. Not because he couldn't do it but,
she was very much afraid, because he *could.*

The outraged sister in her insisted she could resist.
The incredibly aroused woman who'd practically
begged him to take her knew better.

It took a while, but eventually she was able to grasp
the end of the folded-down sheet with her toes and drag
it up her body. A contortionist she wasn't. But by lifting
her legs all the way up in the air and toward her chest,
she managed to drop the covering so it at least reached
her midriff. All the wiggling, jiggling, cursing and bouncing wouldn't bring the blasted thing up over her
breasts, however. So the man was going to get some
peek-a-boo nipple action, but at least nothing farther
south.

She'd just begun contemplating whether she should
hit him before she got dressed, or after, when the door
creaked open.

Jade held her breath, praying it was Ryan, even as
she hated the idea of seeing him again.

"Still here, I see," he said as he came into the room.

She shot him a glare. "Like I was going to be able to
go anywhere?"

He shrugged. "You're very resourceful."

"Resourceful wouldn't help me drag this eigh-
teenth-century cherrywood bed over to the bathroom."

"You needed to go?"

She glared. "No, I hoped I might be able to find something in your shaving kit so I could unlock these things." Then she added, "And maybe a pair of scissors to attack you with."

He quirked a sideways grin, then began to look her over, head to foot. But he didn't get far, his gaze lingering somewhere below the throat. Her standing-at-attention nipples clued her in on where.

She swallowed a lump of rising awareness. "Unlock me."

"Are you going to attack me?"

"Not sexually," she snapped.

"Bummer," he said with a lift of his shoulders. "How about violently?"

"I'm debating."

"On?"

"On how loud it would be if I crack your head open with that lamp on the dressing table."

He glanced at it and tsked. "Porcelain. Pricey. And probably loud. Not to mention that these floors are wood. The thud would probably be heard all the way to your uncle Henry's room."

He was right. And somehow, drat the man, he was making her want to laugh with the matter-of-fact way he was trying to help her figure out how to attack him. Then again, since she was still handcuffed, he did hold a certain position of power.

"Please unlock me."

"I'm making sure you've calmed down," he replied, returning his gaze to her face and staring at her with a kind of quiet intensity he hadn't shown before.

Jade felt heat rise in her body, up her cheeks. The heat inside her was nothing compared to the expression on his face.

He wanted, all right. Still wanted.

"If you won't unlock me, you can certainly be decent enough to pull the sheet all the way up." Sakes alive, even to her own ears, her tone sounded more provocative than pleading.

"Can I?"

His voice was low, almost a purr, as he approached the bed. She couldn't read the look on his face. No smile, no twinkle in his green eyes to help her gauge his intentions.

Was he about to unlock her? Or strip naked and climb into bed beside her? And which was she really, deep in the innermost part of herself, hoping for?

He knelt on the bed, his knee close to her side, pulling the sheet tighter across her tummy and hips. Then he reached up, already holding a small silver key, and unlocked the cuffs.

She immediately pulled her hands free. Lowering her arms, she rubbed her wrists and shrugged her aching shoulders.

"Let me," he said.

"Hands off. Don't try your tricks on me again."

His expression said he was hurt. "I only wanted to ease the knots."

He reached his hands up again as Jade clutched the sheet to cover the front of her body. She had to tug it a little since he was still kneeling on the bed. He shifted, freeing the sheet and also sitting down beside her.

Then, only then, did Jade give a short nod. A shoulder rub was the least the man could do considering he'd caused the discomfort.

He began to stroke her upper arms, kneading, deep strokes that eased the tight muscles there. Then he moved higher, working on her shoulders, his hands moving over her with both strength and gentleness, as if he knew which she needed when. Jade couldn't help relaxing, dropping her head to the side. From behind her, she heard his breathing grow deeper, slower. More intimate.

Oh, so much more intimate.

She wanted that, so very much. But the thought of those hands, those strong, tender hands, having already touched her sister in the same way was just too much.

It wasn't so much about him *hurting* Jenny. It wasn't even about him locking her up naked and disappearing for an hour. Now this had become much more personal, with so much more at stake.

She simply didn't want to sleep with a man who'd been in bed with her sister. Period.

"I can't do this," she said, her voice shaking.

He didn't remove his hands, but they did pause on her shoulders, touching her with gentle possession but demanding nothing.

"I have to go."

He instantly removed his hands and slid off the bed to stand next to her. It took a moment before she could work up the nerve to turn her head and lift her eyes to meet his.

He looked serious. Intense. Maybe even a little sorrowful.

"I understand." He tossed a bag onto the foot of the bed. "Here are your clothes. Maybe…maybe once you can forget about my, uh, getting even tonight, we can meet again. Start over."

Start over. How lovely that sounded. She wished they could, considering he was the first man she'd ever known who'd both aroused her and completely matched her, wit for wit, in a hot, playful game of up the sexual ante. She had to admit it, if only in her mind, she'd liked their games. Ryan could be a very exciting playmate. In bed, and out of it.

If only she could pretend he was just an incredibly attractive man she'd recently met. That there was no baggage, no revenge schemes between them.

No Jenny.

She wanted to wail at the loss. She wanted this man more than she'd ever wanted anyone. In her life.

Sudden frustration rose and she clawed at her clothes, yanking her tank top on over her head, then tugging the sheet out from under it. Staying under the covers, she maneuvered her panties toward her feet and slid into them.

Clad in that much, at least, she felt a little more confident about her ability to face him. She stood up beside the bed. "It's impossible, Ryan."

"Nothing's impossible." His low, hypnotic voice almost made her believe it.

"I can never be with someone I don't trust and respect," she said. "Or someone who doesn't trust and respect me."

His brow shot up and his mouth dropped open. "Trust and respect?" he said, sounding completely offended. "This from the woman who tied me naked to a statue in a public place?"

"It wasn't public," she retorted.

"About as damn close as you can get."

"You said nobody saw you except Tally. And she wasn't wearing her glasses."

His face turned red and he leaned close. "Mamie Brandywine saw me as well. I had to stick like glue to other people leaving the inn this morning so she wouldn't corner me."

She snickered. Mamie's appetites were well known in Savannah. Half the town pitied her husband. The other half wondered what he wasn't doing to keep her satisfied at home.

Such ran the gossip mill.

She reached for her skirt, bunching it and stepping into the waist, still not trusting herself to look at him.

"Why, Jade? Why can't we even try to make something happen when we both know it's what we want?"

"Maybe we could," she replied without thinking about it, "if only you weren't such a womanizing reprobate."

He gave her a look of such shock and confusion that she almost felt sorry for him. The feeling quickly disappeared when he stepped closer, crowding her until the backs of her legs were against the bed. He'd stepped onto the bunched-up fabric of her skirt, so she was stuck there, with her feet inside it and the material puddled around them.

Grabbing her shoulders, he glared at her. "You've got a lot of nerve. I wasn't the one begging you to get naked in the moonlight. You wanna talk about people moving a little fast…"

She blinked. Was that a tiny bit of fear creeping up her spine? A bit of concern at the fury she heard in his voice and saw in his stiff form? Or maybe it was just excitement at seeing his raw masculine power unleashed.

Ryan had been in many moods since they'd met, but she'd never seen him truly angry. "Do you really want to compare notes on who was the aggressor here?" he asked, his voice shaking.

She jerked away from him, forgetting that her feet were tangled. There was only one way to go—down.

She wound up on her butt on the bed, eye level with his waist, and realized his anger hadn't done much to tamp down his arousal.

Wow. Not much at all.

She blinked her eyes and forced herself to look up toward his face. Sticking out her jaw, she hit him with the accusation she'd meant to keep to herself. "I'm not talking about *me*. I'm a grown woman. I know how to take care of myself around smooth-talkers like you."

He leaned over her, so close she could see the crisp black hairs in the open vee of his black cotton shirt. See the sheen of sweat on his skin and the bunching of his muscles. Slick. Bulging. Powerful. She gulped and tore her stare away.

Fisting his hands, Ryan bent close and put them on either side of her on the mattress, effectively trapping her. "You're not making any sense. You don't know a thing about me. Not about my past, who I've dated. Nothing."

"I know about Jenny," she snapped, trying to keep her wits about her when what she wanted to do was ask him if he knew there were tiny flecks of gold scattered across the green of his eyes. She regretted it as soon as the words left her mouth.

"Who?"

She tried to backpedal. "Never mind."

"No, I do mind. What aren't you telling me?"

"Look, it doesn't matter." Forcing a laugh, she tried to change the subject. "Why are we arguing anyway? It's not that big a deal never to see each other again. You can't want *me* too much if you had me naked and chained to a bed and still walked out the door."

This time, he was the one who barked a laugh. A disbelieving grunt of a laugh. "Not want you? Babe, a man would have to be gay, castrated at birth or had his nads blown off in an industrial accident not to have wanted you."

She sucked her lips into her mouth, both amused and a little mollified at the tormented tone in his voice. Okay, walking out hadn't been easy. That was a relief.

He straightened and crossed his arms, but remained threateningly close, as if silently ordering her to stay seated. "I did it to teach you a lesson about playing games with men you don't know."

"Yeah?" she said, scoffing at him with her tone. "Well, maybe I did that to you for the same reason."

He quirked a brow. "I don't play games with men."

"I sure hope not."

"So what makes you think I play games with women? Go back to what you were saying earlier—about Jenny."

She didn't want to, didn't mean to, didn't plan to. But somehow the words burst out of her anyway. "Jenny Maguire, from New York? She's my sister."

He continued to stare, then nodded slowly. "The waitress who wants to be an actress?"

He didn't even try to deny it, the dog. "Yeah. I guess she got some great acting lessons from you. How to act like you have a heart."

His jaw tightened and the amusement left his face. "Since I only met the girl twice in my life, I don't know what the hell you're talking about."

"Of course you know what I'm talk..." Then she paused as his words sunk in. "Twice?"

"Yeah, twice. Once in the diner where she worked. Once when we went out for lunch. Twice. End of story."

"Twice," she repeated dumbly, wondering what to believe, who to trust. "Jenny said she...she cared for you."

He ran a hand wearily through his hair, rumpling those dark waves into a sexy, bed-tousled disarray. "I don't know what she told you, Jade. But here's the truth. I met her at the diner when she waited on me. I invited her to lunch at one of those tourist traps where you sit in a stage-shaped booth. We ate. We talked. We had our picture taken. We left. I've never seen or spoken to her again."

"Why not?"

"Good grief, she's got to be all of what? Twenty? And I'm supposed to have developed some great passion for her? This is nuts!"

"So why'd you ask her to lunch in the first place?" she shot back.

For the first time, Ryan looked away. He thrust his hands into the pockets of his jeans. Through the worn blue fabric, she could see his fingers curl into fists. "It was a bad idea at a bad moment." He looked up at her through half-lowered lashes, his frown screaming his discomfort at the topic of conversation. "Haven't you ever had a bad idea?"

Oh, good heavens, yes. Like tracking down this guy. Getting involved with him. Getting him naked and tying him up to a little winged cherub statue. And getting herself naked and handcuffed to his bed...*without* him in it.

"I seem to have had nothing *but* bad ideas at bad moments since you and I met," she admitted.

They both fell silent for a long moment. Jade didn't look at him. She merely looked at her hands, trembling against her bare thighs. That slight trembling told her more about her emotional state than her own brain had been able to.

Jenny had lied. Or at least exaggerated. She didn't

seem to recognize the difference. Never had, probably never would.

Once again, the drama queen at the center of her own drama.

The next time she saw her spoiled sibling, Jade was going to have to make her work on that. Or else just slap her silly.

Ryan remained standing a few feet away, obviously as lost in thought as she. "So you thought I was involved with your sister," he finally said.

She corrected him. "I thought you *hurt* my sister. And I was out to, um…correct the injustice."

He merely shook his head. "I'd hate to see how you correct the injustice if someone actually harmed *you*."

She shrugged. "I wouldn't. I can take care of myself. At least usually." She glanced at the handcuffs.

He met her eye, understanding her meaning. Jade wasn't vengeful, not on her own behalf, anyway. But damned if anyone was going to hurt anyone she cared about.

"Point taken," he finally replied.

Then it was her turn to understand. "You thought I was some sick woman who liked picking up men and humiliating them for no reason, which is why you paid me back tonight. Here." She looked at the bed and softly added, "Like this."

"Yeah. We really made a mess of things, didn't we?" he asked.

"A major mess. I'd say this one would have to go in the record books for strange starts to relationships."

"Relationships?" His tone was hopeful. Or maybe Jade just read hope in his voice because she wanted it to be there.

Forgetting that her skirt was tangled around her

feet, she tried to stand up but immediately stumbled. It certainly wasn't by design that she landed right against his body, his warm, *welcoming* body.

His arms instantly reached to steady her, one hand landing below her waist, the other on her arm. Only a tiny scrap of elastic separated his hand from her bare hip and the skin there instantly felt hot and tender.

"What have we done?" he whispered, looking at her for answers she didn't have either.

"We certainly started out all wrong. But we started *something*," she said, not sure where the words had come from but knowing they were the right ones. And she knew, without a doubt, it was something she wanted to continue.

His thumb slid beneath the elastic, caressing her hip-bone. The fingers of his other hand scraped delicately up her arm, to her shoulder, then to the nape of her neck.

"So where do we go from here?" He stepped even closer, his warm breath touching her hair as he continued to caress her gently with his fingertips.

"We could go the normal route. You ask me to dinner. I say yes and play hard to get when you walk me to the door."

He continued to delicately touch her neck, so lightly she wondered if she was feeling his fingertips or a bit of breeze stirred up by the lazily turning ceiling fan.

"Considering we've seen each other naked and touched each other as intimately as lovers, I'd say the normal route's a bit of a step backward," he murmured.

She already knew that and was glad he concurred. She hesitated for no longer than a heartbeat. Her voice wasn't the least bit uncertain when she replied. "Okay, then, now I guess we make love."

8

RYAN HAD PICTURED HAVING sex with Jade from the moment he'd first laid eyes on her. His desire for her, mixed with his anger at what she'd done, had filled his mind constantly. Nearly every waking thought had been full of hot sexual images where lust and hunger merged with anger and revenge until he couldn't think of anything else.

His nighttime mind hadn't been much different. Crazy, wicked dreams he hadn't experienced since he was a kid had left him trembling in his bed the previous night. And had left him wondering if he was really capable of doing the things to and with her that he'd dreamt of.

This, however, this moment which had finally arrived, was *nothing* like that. He didn't know who was more surprised—he or Jade—that the crazy anger and palpable heat had somehow evaporated, leaving in their place a kind of sweet, aching need that he'd never felt before.

Tonight was suddenly about nothing other than pure desire. He wasn't prompted by anger, but rather by a completely unexpected feeling of languorous want.

Even more amazing, he didn't hate himself for wanting her so much, knowing about her what he did. Instead, he gave himself over to it, glad he had the chance before she slipped out of his life—as quickly as she'd slipped into it. She was like a dark, sleek cat, one you spotted in the moonlight moving through the shadows until it disappeared out of sight. And then you wondered, long after it was gone, if you'd ever really seen it at all.

He didn't want her to disappear. To her real life, to her crazy family or her strange apartment or her life of crime.

He wanted her here. Now. In his arms. For at least one night.

"Ryan?" she whispered, sounding as confused as he felt. Amazingly, the mindless fury had evaporated, leaving them both wrapped in a kind of warm, sultry comfort that spoke of long slow loving on a hot summer night.

That's what he wanted. More than anything else. He wanted a sultry, slow, unhurried and completely sensual night of lovemaking with Jade Maguire—a woman he'd been prepared to hate. But one he'd come to understand much better in the twenty-four hours since they'd met. Particularly after his conversation with her unusual great-aunt, who hadn't helped him as far as the painting went, but *had* made him realize he didn't know the whole story.

She'd convinced him that he should give Jade a chance to prove him wrong about her. The old woman had encouraged him to get closer to Jade in order to understand the things she did, the choices she made. He had the feeling Lula Mae had meant *more* than understanding why Jade might have become a thief.

That issue remained for later. Not now.

"Jade," he whispered, drawing out her name on a

long, exhaled breath. "How can you make me so insane and yet so calmly certain all in a single night?"

Her eyes widened in surprise, then in understanding. So he felt it, too—something had changed for both of them.

Jade seemed to have dropped her guard, looking like the beautiful, charming young woman he'd glimpsed a few times since they'd met. The defenses were down, perhaps because she'd learned he hadn't hurt her sister.

He didn't question tomorrow, which would dawn with the same myriad of problems they'd had since the moment they'd met. But tonight wasn't about those things. It was just about *this*. This world the two of them had created, and which they now had to explore fully. This was the only thing he felt certain of.

A slow smile widened his lips as he reached one hand out to gently cup her waist. He didn't pull her toward him. He didn't drive her back onto the bed and let the subdued passion between them erupt into the final conflagration they'd both probably have predicted an hour ago. Instead he moved toward her mouth, her beautiful, perfect mouth, going slowly enough to give her the chance to turn away, if she wished to do so.

She didn't move, merely waited, anticipation gleaming in her eyes and a soft sigh the only sound as his lips brushed hers.

"Stay with me tonight," he whispered, gently licking at her lips until they parted for him. Then their tongues met in a slow, lazy exploration. The kiss told him, more than anything else, that she'd experienced a change in mood which matched his own.

"I'm not going anywhere," she confirmed, her voice husky but a little stunned.

He understood how she felt—suddenly unsure of

something that had seemed straightforward a few minutes ago. This hadn't happened to him before. His relationships usually started out frenzied and picked up steam. He'd never wanted to slow down and savor every step of a first exploration. Never. Not like this.

"I don't want you handcuffed to my bed," he whispered, moving to kiss the corner of her mouth, then the fine line of her jaw. Then he laughed lightly. "At least not *yet.*"

She moaned and arched her head back, twining her fingers in his hair and caressing his earlobe. "What *do* you want?"

Easy one. "I want to touch every inch of you. Feel your skin and wonder again how it can be softer than any flower I've ever touched. And how you can smell more intoxicating."

She moaned, reaching up to slip her arms around his neck and tug him to her for another kiss. Ryan complied, sipping of her mouth, tasting the unique combination of sweet and spicy that so perfectly described the woman in his arms.

Their clothes came off slowly. He was sliding Jade's black tank up and over her shoulders almost before he realized he was doing it. They parted for a moment so he could pull it over her head. After tossing it to the floor, he moved in for another deep, wet kiss. He couldn't resist touching that supple skin, and he smoothed his palms up her sides until he could cup both of her breasts. She shivered a little, then pressed against him as he teased her dark, taut nipples with his fingertips.

"You're so beautiful," he whispered as he looked down at her, clad in nothing but her lacy black panties. "You're not going to walk out on me this time?"

He shook his head, knowing he'd sooner put a gun to his head than walk out now, before finishing what they'd started the previous night in the garden. Hell, even *earlier*. This intensity had been building since their first look.

She seemed to believe him because she immediately reached for his shirt, tugging it free from his jeans. She pushed it up, her hands doing crazy, heavenly things to his chest and shoulders on the way.

"Wait," he said when she reached for his waistband. He had to feel her, skin to skin, first. So he drew her closer, groaning in pleasure when her nipples scraped his chest. She rubbed back and forth lightly, touching him with nothing but those two sensitive spots. Sucking in a slow breath between her teeth, she heightened the tension for both of them by teasing her own puckered skin with the hair of his chest.

Then she grasped his shoulders, her whole body shaking a little in reaction. The shaking, that hint of unsteadiness—as if she had no more power to resist what was happening between them than a flower could resist the sun—sent a surge of pure male satisfaction through him.

"Why do I feel like I've been building up to this all my life instead of just a few minutes?"

He shook his head and tsked. "We've been building up to this for more than twenty-four hours."

She shrugged, conceding his point, then reached for his waistband. She made short work of his jeans, unfastening them and pushing them off his hips. Ryan's breath caught in his throat when she tugged his briefs away, trailing her hand across the tip of his erection in a move too teasing to be accidental.

"I can't wait, and yet I don't even want to start because I don't want it to be over," she said, her voice choked with desire and a hint of desperate laughter.

"Ditto. So I should probably tell you," he said, "I haven't gone six times in one night in a long time." Then he gave her a sideways grin. "However, I have to admit, something's sparking inside me tonight. I'm feeling unstoppable." His own wolfish chuckle startled him. Wondering where this incredible surge of both sexual energy and sexual patience had come from, he added, "And *very* potent."

She laughed until their mouths met in another deep kiss full of shared breaths and tongue-tangling passion. Their kisses grew deeper and wetter. Then all clothes were gone, disappearing beneath frantic hands.

They gently fell onto the bed, still wrapped around one another, exchanging kiss after kiss. Each touch sucked Ryan deeper into a well of physical pleasure until he was sure he'd drown in it. Drown in her.

Unable to resist anymore, he slid his fingers into that hot, wet flesh between her legs, teasing those soft, pretty curls, feeling her shudder in response.

"So wet," he groaned as he played with her slick opening. He toyed with her, gauging her responses, filling her tight heat with one finger, then another, until she began to gasp and writhe. And finally he flicked at her pert little clit until her whole body shook and she began to beg in tiny whimpers and pleas.

"Ryan, do you have any protection?" she managed to bite out between gasps.

"Yeah," he said, needing every bit of control he had to pull away and reach toward the bedside table. "This wasn't planned, but I sure wasn't going to take any chances."

"Just in case?" she asked, amusement blending with the stark hunger in her eyes.

"Just in case."

Then he sheathed himself and slid into her warm, welcoming body. Jade rocked up to meet him, lifting her legs, taking him deeper.

He should have known she'd be as passionate in bed as she was about everything else. She wrapped her legs around his hips and her arms around his shoulders, already starting to gasp and breathe hard. He ground against her, seeing the unmistakable signs that she was, incredibly, already close to the edge.

"Oh, yes," she murmured, "I've been thinking about this since last night. Please…a little more…oooh."

Then she stretched, arched her back, and shook slightly. Ryan waited, watching, seeing the flush of color rise in her beautiful cheeks and her lips part as she sucked in shallow breaths. Her wildly tangled black hair provided exactly the contrast to his white sheets that he'd pictured when he'd first seen her. But having her here, in his arms, with their bodies together, exceeded anything he could have imagined.

She was tight and wet and hot and in the throes of pleasure. No way could he stop himself from moving.

Her eyes flew open. "Yes. Yes. You need to catch up."

He chuckled at her demanding tone and sunk into her again, deeper, until she gasped and twisted her hips to accommodate him. "I didn't mean to get ahead of you," she said between choppy breaths. "I'm not usually so, um…quick…."

"I don't feel left behind." He pulled out of her slowly, feeling the exquisite sensation not only in his groin but everywhere else in his body. "As long as you're not really *finished* when you reach that finish line, I don't consider this a race at all."

Smiling, she pulled his face down for another kiss. "I feel so sorry for men," she said, sounding anything but as she squeezed him deep inside her body, eliciting a guttural groan from his throat. "You only get to cross the finish line once."

He gave her an evil look. "We'll see about that." He felt completely up to the challenge of a long, erotic night.

She surprised him by suddenly pushing at his chest, rolling him over and climbing on top. He stared up at her, loving this sight most of all. Jade, her hair wild and loose around her face, her lips swollen from his kisses, looking down at him with pure feminine pleasure.

She rocked on him, taking and giving, and he rose up to meet her every downward stroke.

"This is good," she said hoarsely. She reached up to cup her own breasts. Ryan moaned at the sight, then tugged her close to capture one dark nipple between his lips. He sucked deeply, feeling her jerk against him in response.

He suckled harder as she set the pace she needed. When her breathing grew frantic, he held her hips, taking over from below while she came again in a blaze of glorious, satisfied cries. Then she collapsed on his chest, trying to regain her breath but still joined with him.

"You know, I believe this Southern air—or Southern *tea*," he said, remembering the brew Lula Mae gave him, "is doing me some good." He stroked her hair and her smooth back. "Because I think I'm going to have to watch you do that at least a half-dozen more times tonight."

"Deal," she whispered as she licked at his chest.

Rolling over, she dug her fingers into his hips, her whole body straining up toward him as he entered her again.

Nothing felt this good. Had *ever* felt this good.

"Maybe we'd better make that an even dozen," he said as he gave himself over to the pleasure they created once again.

And by the early predawn hours, he realized he hadn't missed by much.

JADE WOKE UP FIRST the next morning, unused to the long, hard body curled up against her back. When her cat, Jinx, curled up against her, he was usually right beside her face where, Aunt Lula Mae often said, he could steal her breath.

This definitely wasn't Jinx. No, this warmth wasn't soft in any way. It was all hard. Solid. Strong.

After a moment and a rapid blink of her eyes, she remembered where she was. And with whom.

It was true. She'd spent the night in Ryan Stoddard's bed, in a room at Uncle Henry's inn. All those lovely dreams of someone worshipping her, cherishing her, kissing every inch of her and making love to her until she couldn't remember her own name hadn't been dreams.

He'd made them real.

She closed her eyes, taking in a deep breath as she remembered their long, erotic night. She'd never experienced anything like it. She didn't imagine many women did.

"Perfect," she whispered, then she smiled.

Seeing the pinkish-gray light of a new morning sky slanting in through the center of the heavy drapes, she held out hope that she could get out of here without being seen. She didn't want to have to explain this. Not yet. Maybe because she didn't completely understand what had happened herself.

Carefully turning around until she was face to face with her sleeping lover, she studied him carefully. The long lashes resting on his cheeks. The tiny scar on the bridge of his nose. The shadow of morning stubble on his cheeks. His curved mouth, with those perfect lips slightly parted.

The sheet was tangled around his legs and she took the opportunity to look further. Her breaths grew deeper as she saw the visible proof of the strength she'd felt last night. The cut of muscles in his arm, the ripples in his chest—no wonder he'd carried her so effortlessly. She noted another small scar above one rib—she'd felt that during the night. Then lower. Oh, yes, she'd felt *that*, too.

She knew his body intimately, but she didn't really know the man. She wanted to, though. Desperately.

Jade had never in her life had a one-night stand. Something deep inside her rebelled against the idea that this might have been one. She wanted to laugh with him and talk with him in the moonlight again. Wanted to give him hell for the ridiculous costume he'd worn last night on the tour.

But to what end? He lived in another state. In another world, really. His life was as foreign to her as if he'd come from outer space. She should let him go. Kiss him goodbye. Be content with the few incredible memories they'd created. Geography said they had no future, even if her heart—along with other more *tender* body parts—was saying she should try to find out.

She still hadn't decided what to do when he opened

his eyes and smiled. That crooked smile made his eyes crinkle and spark with light, his lean face turn boyish and playful, and sucked the breath right out of her lungs.

How could she have thought she could just walk away?

"Morning," he growled.

"Good morning."

He pulled her close, draping an arm around her waist. "What are you thinking?"

She wasn't about to tell him the truth. "I was wondering what time it is."

"Too early. Go back to sleep." Then he lazily caressed her hip, teasing the upper curve of her bottom. "Better yet, let's stay awake."

She chuckled. "You're insatiable. I have to go to work."

"You're staying," he said, sounding supremely confident.

"No."

He leaned closer, kissed the tip of her nose and whispered, "Yes."

Her response was slightly weaker than before. "No."

When his hand moved up to cover her breast, tweaking her nipple into instant awareness, she gave a soft, helpless moan.

"Yes," he said again, dropping his mouth to her throat. "Yes." He nibbled his way lower. Then, *oh, God,* lower.

She groaned in anticipation, seeing his head between her legs, knowing the pleasure he wanted to give her. "Yes," he whispered once more before his tongue began to do incredibly wild and wicked things to her, making her gasp and whimper.

He toyed and nibbled and licked at her until she lost control and shook as hot waves of intense pleasure roared through her entire body.

Then once more he ordered her to give herself over to him, to let him have his way. "Yes."

She could no longer even try to resist. "Yes."

Two hours later, however, she refused to allow him to coax her into staying. It was 8:00 a.m., and she could hear people moving around the house. She hoped she could escape while Uncle Henry visited with his guests during breakfast.

"When can I see you again?" Ryan asked as she emerged from the bathroom pulling her top on over her head.

He watched her from the bed, the sheet draped across his lap. Looking at him, she forgot to move for a second, with her head stuck out of her tank top and her arms tangled inside it. His thick arms, tousled hair and crooked smile had her wanting to crawl right back between the sheets and spend the day doing everything all over again.

Lord, she was becoming a sex maniac.

She finally remembered what the heck she'd been doing and pulled the top in place, then reached for her skirt.

"You, uh, want to see me again?" she asked, cursing the little squeak in her voice. Hopefully he hadn't heard it.

No such luck. He rose from the bed, striding toward her, his body lean and powerful. Her mouth went dry remembering the feel of him on top of her. Beneath her. Inside her. She closed her eyes, then opened them again.

"You're damn right I do," he said, taking her jaw in his hand. "I don't know what last night was about for you, but it was only a beginning for me."

A beginning. Of something that wasn't likely to have a happy ending. A wiser woman would have backed away, ended things now. Jade had always considered herself pretty smart. But as Aunt Lula Mae often said, particularly about Jade's mama, "Da heart don' always like to listen to what da head has to say."

"All right," she whispered.

His relieved smile was gratifying. "Spend the day with me."

"I just spent the night with you."

"So the rest will be easy."

She nibbled her lip. "I have to work."

"Aren't you the boss?"

She nodded. "But I have to do some things. Including going home and checking on Aunt Lula Mae." She looked down at her shirt and crumpled skirt. "Not to mention changing clothes."

"Then spend the afternoon with me."

"I can't."

He got out of the bed and approached her. Jade threw her hand up, palm out. "Don't try to persuade me."

He gave her an innocent, "who me?" look, and kept right on walking, until he was flush against her. Neck to knee. Breath to breath. "Meet me this afternoon."

"I ca…."

He kissed the end of the word right out of her mouth, taking her lips against his and licking his way inside so he could tease her tongue into saying yes.

"Say yes," he whispered when they drew apart.

"Do you always get your way?"

He nodded. "Always."

At least the man was honest. "All right. Just this afternoon. But no more playing hooky for me—I have a business to run."

He put two fingers straight up in the air and vowed, "Absolutely. Just today."

She didn't trust the humor in his eyes.

"And the next day."

"Ryan…"

"And the day after that."

She was laughing as she left the room. Laughing, and suspecting he might be right.

"So, who's the guy?"

Jade looked up from her desk the next morning, seeing Daisy framed in the doorway of her downtown office. Her all-black clothes and stark white makeup looked especially out of place on such a bright, beautiful summer day.

"I don't know what you mean," she replied, nibbling her lip at the lie.

Daisy smirked and entered the small, one-room office that Jade had rented last year when the record-keeping and phone calls had become too much to handle at home. She plopped down on the seat opposite the desk. "You are so full of it. I know you, Jade. This is the 'I-got-laid Jade' I'm seeing here."

Jade couldn't prevent a tiny smile. Daisy was so outrageous, but also a very intuitive friend. Jade had definitely gotten laid. Oh boy, oh boy, oh boy, had she!

"I think we're supposed to be talking about you and, uh, your formerly incarcerated friend," she replied, forcing her mind out of the bed she'd been sharing with Ryan for the past couple of nights.

Daisy shrugged. "I dunno. It's okay, except all he ever wants to talk about is how bad it was inside without a real fast-food burger for eighteen months. All we've done is hit every drive-thru in Savannah. Cripes, you'd think the key to getting some psycho to confess to anything is withholding his daily Whopper."

Jade met Daisy's eyes, they shared a salacious look, and both burst into laughter.

"Okay, so other than being sick of fast-food, what else is going on?"

Daisy shrugged. "He's changed. Or I've changed. Whatever. We just don't seem to have much in common anymore. He's even mentioned wanting to go back to Iowa and live off his folks on the farm. I'd rather have somebody stick flaming toothpicks up my nose than do that."

"Lovely," Jade murmured.

"I don't know if we'll make it. Seems kind of silly since I moved all the way up here to be close to the prison."

As much as she'd hate losing Daisy, Jade would much rather have the girl get the loser ex out of her life. "You don't want to go back to New Orleans, do you?"

Daisy crossed her arms across her chest, leaned back in her chair and lifted one boot-covered foot onto her other knee. "Nah. I've gotten used to it here in Savannah. Genteel freaky instead of raunchy freaky."

Jade nodded in rueful agreement. That kind of summed things up.

"So, tell me about your guy. Who put that look on your face?" Daisy asked, not distracted from her original question.

"What look?" The I-met-an-amazing-man-and-we've-spent-nearly-every-minute-together-for-the-last-two-days look?

She swallowed hard and lifted her water bottle to her lips, still trying to divert Daisy's attention. The water had been here all morning and was now somewhere between tepid and bathwater, but it was better than having to try to explain the crazy relationship she'd fallen into with a practical stranger.

An amazingly delicious relationship, but a crazy one nonetheless.

"Spill," said Daisy.

"It's not a big deal."

Daisy reached over and helped herself to a handful of peanut M&M's, which Jade kept in a dish on her desk. She picked out all the green ones, munched them, and dumped the others back in the bowl. "Puh-lease. You got some, I can see it all over you."

Jade quirked a brow and pointed to her loose yellow skirt and sleeveless top. "In case you haven't noticed, I'm not wearing a dress from the Gap."

Quick-witted Daisy immediately got Jade's Monica Lewinsky reference and snorted a laugh. "Is it anybody I know?"

Jade shook her head knowing she might as well come clean. Daisy was like a kid digging through a cereal box for a toy. Relentless, thorough, and not caring what spilled onto the floor. "He's someone I just met. And we're..."

"Having wild sex?"

"We're getting to know one another."

"In bed."

"And out," Jade shot back.

Daisy chortled. "Aha, so there was a bed in there somewhere!"

Oh, yes. A bed. A garden. The bathtub at the hotel Ryan had checked into yesterday afternoon—not wanting to stay at another cozy B&B where Jade was well-known.

She didn't mind people knowing she had sex—most people made a regular practice of it. She *did* mind people hearing anything, um, unusual from another room, in an old house with more old layers of paint than nails holding up the walls.

One thing was for sure—whether it was the Southern air or something else— Ryan was definitely the most potent man she'd ever known. His appetites perfectly matched hers.

They were both insatiable.

Ryan. Just thinking about him made her feel the most unusual feeling of elation. Jade had considered herself much too…well, *jaded* ever to turn into one of those giddy women who gauged their happiness by the barometer of their love life. Like her mother and her sister.

Her sister. That had been an interesting conversation. She'd called Jenny yesterday morning when she'd gone home for a change of clothes. Jenny had been rattling on about auditions and a big tipper at the restaurant. When Jade had asked about Ryan, her sister had responded with an unexpected, "Who?"

A few more words and Jenny had confirmed she'd blown a lunch date into gargantuan proportions.

Typical Jenny, their mother's daughter. A whirling bundle of energy who loved being at the center of attention and treated every aspect of her life as if she were the star performer and everyone else merely supporting players.

Jade was much more like her father. Danny Maguire had been a black-haired Irishman whose stoicism had hidden a deeply vulnerable emotional side. Not that he'd often let anyone see it. He'd been the stable element in their family. He'd put up with Mama's flamboyance and with two outrageously different daughters. He'd never protested the presence of a live-in great-aunt—a voodoo priestess who wasn't even technically a blood relation, since Lula Mae had been adopted by Jade's great-grandfather decades ago.

He'd done it all with quiet wisdom and a good-natured laugh. Right up until the end when he was dying of the kind of cancer that brought men to their knees, robbing them of life long before it actually killed them. Even now, more than twelve years later, she missed him every day. Tears rose in her eyes, as they always did when she thought about him.

Jade had been thinking about him a good deal over the past few days, and she didn't question why. It was because she'd finally begun to wonder if she was like her mother after all, able to experience love strong enough to last a lifetime. Hungry for love, wanting it desperately. Not because she'd *lost* it, as Patty Jean had, but because she'd never truly experienced it at all.

So far.

She couldn't imagine what Daddy would be thinking of her latest situation. Little Miss Common Sense, involved in a passionate affair with a man whose address she didn't even know. He'd be surprised, she was sure, because she'd been described from childhood as the calm, introspective, thoughtful one. The one who never let her emotions rule her head. Just like Daddy.

"You okay?" Daisy asked, interrupting Jade's long moments of silent thought. "The sex was so good that you're still crying over it a day later? Or was it that *bad*?"

Jade quickly wiped at the tears she hadn't realized

were there and was about to reply when she realized someone else had entered the office. Her nerve endings all perked up in reaction, so she knew before even looking who it was.

Ryan.

9

"SHE'S DEFINITELY NOT crying because it was bad," Ryan said with the kind of casual confidence some men never achieved in their entire lives. He strode into her office, filling up the small space with his mere presence.

Even Daisy did a double-take—and she was tough to impress.

"Well, hello," she said. "I think we were just talking about you. Brought out the emotional side of Jade."

Never one to allow anyone to be too sure of her, Jade merely shrugged. "I had something in my eye."

Ryan crossed the room in a few steps and looked down at Jade with visible concern. "You're sure? Is anything wrong?"

"Yeah," Daisy said, standing up and crossing her arms in front of her chest. "She's crying because she's finally realized all she missed out on by not having sex for a couple of years."

Oh, man. Jade was really going to kill her now. "Go away."

Ryan looked amused. "Years?"

".I'm gone." Daisy gave Ryan a thorough once-over, nodded and winked her approval, then sauntered toward the door.

Before she escaped, Jade came up with a decent

comeback. "You're one to talk considering where your boyfriend's been for the past year and a half!"

Daisy gave her a half smile and Jade realized that probably hadn't been the right retort. The young woman didn't seem the type to wait around for eighteen months for any man.

God, she felt old. Though only twenty-six to Daisy's nineteen, she'd played the mother to Jenny for so long that she didn't remember *ever* being as reckless as the younger women.

"Years?" Ryan asked again once Daisy was gone.

"She was exaggerating."

He waited.

"Greatly."

Still waited.

"Not *years*, plural."

Then he sat on the corner of her desk, looking completely at ease in his casual jeans and T-shirt as he waited for more details. He wasn't getting them. Instead, she went on the offensive. "Want to talk about *your* previous sex life?"

"Nope."

"Then don't ask about mine."

Boring as it's been.

He bent down and gave her a quick, possessive kiss on the lips. "Not talking about former sex lives. That's a sign of a relationship, isn't it?"

"There's that word again."

"Sex?"

"Relationship," she retorted. "That's not what we have."

He got off the desk and squatted next to her. Swiveling her around, he pulled the rolling chair closer until her knees touched his chest and his hands covered hers. "We don't have to put a name on it, Jade."

Good.

"But we both know we've fallen into something."

Fallen in. Naked, tied and handcuffed, but definitely fallen. "It's not like it can go anywhere," she said, determined not to get attached to this man and the things he made her feel.

"Why not?"

He looked really curious and a little confused, as if he hadn't noticed the minor problems of geography and their vastly different lifestyles. He was a responsible big-city architect who worked with millionaires on renovating their Fifth Avenue penthouses. She was a two-paychecks-away-from-broke tour guide operator who scared tourists for a living.

"We don't seem to have much common ground," she finally said, considering it the understatement of a lifetime.

His evil grin told her his mind had gone right into his pants.

"Other than that," she added, a laugh on her lips.

Oh, yeah, they had *that*. They had sexual compatibility coming out the yin-yang. But they didn't have anything else.

So they'd managed to fill a day or two and enjoy each other's company out of bed, as well. He liked her kind of music. She liked his kind of buildings. They both liked sushi and loathed catfish. They had fun window-shopping on River Street and liked people-watching in the Victorian District.

That didn't mean they were compatible, or anything. He was strictly northeastern white-bread conservative and she was Southern mixed-race bohemian.

"I can't believe I let you talk me into taking another afternoon off," she muttered as she led him outside and locked up the office.

"You're the perfect guide for these old plantation houses."

"And you're relentless about getting what you want. You must have driven your parents crazy, you spoiled brat."

He shrugged, unrepentant. "You like getting your own way, too. You're just a little more *genteel* about it."

True. She did like getting her own way. She'd had to. She'd been pretty much in charge of her little family since she was a teenager, and had become used to her mother following her advice. "Okay, so we're both used to being the boss. Both oldest kids—"

"And oldest grandkids," he added.

"Correct. We both like to be the one in the driver's seat."

He leaned close to her ear. "Right. And sometimes we both want to be on top. But I think we've managed to compromise and work things out there, don't you?"

Oh, lordy, she had set herself up for that one. She gulped, pushed a long strand of hair off her face and ordered herself not to blush. Not now, when other business owners she knew were walking by, nodding their hellos as she stood there, getting wet and aroused because of this man's wicked whisper.

"We have already established sexual compatibility," she conceded, keeping her voice low. "I'm talking about elsewhere. We don't have much else in common."

He rolled his eyes and made a sound of disgust. "We don't know that. Why do you think I've been insisting you spend your days with me? So we could get to know each other better. Like today, we'll be seeing headstones and houses full of dead people when what I want to do is go back into your office, lift you on top of your desk, flip up your little skirt and take you right there in front of Savannah and the world. Because maybe if I come inside you, again, you'll begin to believe there's something real happening between us."

She dropped her purse—literally dropped it out of her weak fingers—and stood there staring up at him, wide-eyed, on the sidewalk. Two women walked by, women she recognized. They giggled, then one of them picked up her handbag and put it in Jade's shaking fingers.

"Have a nice day, y'hear? 'Bye, honey," she said after giving Ryan a thorough head-to-toe examination. Then the women moved on.

Jade still couldn't say a word.

Finally, he tipped her gaping jaw closed with his index finger. "Do we go back in your office?" he asked, one brow quirked. "Or do we go visit those old museums you so love?"

Swallowing the first answer, the impulsive one from the deepest, most sensual part of her, she snapped, "Let's go."

WHILE DRIVING OUT OF Savannah for their day visiting historic houses of the South, Ryan and Jade maintained a comfortable silence. The hum of the engine droned beneath the hiss of the air conditioner, which tried to bring the stifling outside air to a breathable temperature. Her hand rested on the seat, his close to it, so that just their pinkies touched. That slight touch told him she'd forgiven him for the sexy taunt outside her office.

Hell, he was the one who'd lived to regret it. It'd

taken ten minutes of their drive for him to will his hard-on back down.

The tension was gone, though the awareness remained. There was more, though. If anyone had told him a few days ago that he could be falling for this woman, Ryan would have laughed in that person's face. But it was true. Somewhere between the sex and the anger, the schemes and the desire, they'd started to enjoy one another. To like one another. And, at least on his part, maybe more.

How twisted was that? He cared for a woman he believed was a thief. He was intrigued by her like he'd never been intrigued by anyone. He liked her intelligence and her caustic wit, her smile and her dark, mysterious eyes. Even the hint of vulnerability she'd hate to have anyone notice.

He'd noticed. He'd paid attention to the slight weariness in her shoulders after she'd worked out this weekend's tour schedule last night in his bed. The wistful tone in her voice when she spoke of missing her mother and sister told him more about her than any conversation about their families could have. The sadness when she spoke of the father she'd lost at such a young age broke his heart a little. The exasperated fondness when Lula Mae's name came up merely cemented what he'd figured the night he'd met the old woman.

Jade was the glue that held them all together. He knew that now, without ever having met most of her family. And he liked her even more for it.

None of it reconciled with a deceitful con woman who'd steal from the elderly. None. So he had decided to do exactly what Lula Mae had told him to—get closer to Jade. Much closer. And try to either win her trust, so she'd confide in him, or figure out all on his own how her mind worked.

"So why did you want to go on this field trip today, anyway? Aren't there enough old houses in the city for you to explore?" She shot him an amused look. "Or are you just trying to get away from Mamie Brandywine? She has to have tracked you down by now."

He grimaced. "She left a message for me at the hotel."

"She's relentless."

"She's a hundred and two."

"More like sixty."

"Who could tell?" he asked, wanting to change the subject to a much more pleasant one. "Besides, today gives me a chance to be alone with you, with no cell phone, no pager, no tourists recognizing you and asking questions about where to visit."

She reached to turn up the AC and a thick blast of cold air emerged from the vents. Jade leaned toward it, almost cooing her appreciation. She was such a creature of her senses, and watching the delight she took in so many things drove him crazy. She savored rich smells, decadent desserts, sultry whispers, or coolness against her overheated body.

His touch.

Ryan swallowed hard, knowing he had to get a grip before he drove off the road.

"We've been alone for the past two nights," she said, one brow lifted as she gave him a secretive smile.

So much for getting a grip. That comment put his brain right back into his lap. "I'm gonna get into a wreck if we start talking about the past two nights."

"They were fabulous."

Witch.

"It's a good thing it's not possible to overdose on orgasms, because I'd be a dead woman right now."

He growled and shifted again. "Shut. Up. Jade."

She giggled. "Just getting even for what you said back in front of my office. But I'll shut up now."

Unfortunately, it was too late. Her comments had his mind focused only on the hot, sensual encounters they'd shared. He could not get enough of her. No matter how many times he touched her, his hands felt empty when she wasn't in them.

He'd half wondered if her Aunt Lula Mae had slipped something into his tea that first night. But whatever the spell had been, it hadn't worn off, hadn't decreased in intensity at all. She was all he thought about while awake, all he dreamed about when asleep.

"Well," he said, trying to change the subject to a safer one, "the nights have been *private*. But yesterday was a little crowded."

"Crowded?"

He nodded. "Everyone knows you. Everywhere we went, people have been asking you questions, wanting your advice. I can barely exchange ten words with you before we're interrupted."

From vendors selling brightly-colored T-shirts to sweaty tourists, to artists peddling ten-dollar caricatures, she stopped to talk to them all. Old and young. Male and female. She had a ready smile, a word of support, an answer for every question.

"That happens in a place like this. You see the skyline and think we're a big city. But when you walk the old squares, you know it's still a very small town."

"Still seems strange to me," he said with a shrug.

"There's a whole history here," she said. "So many families have been here for a long time. We grew up to-

gether. Went to school together. Went to the same birthday parties and the same Southern colleges. Lifelong
friends who grow up, marry and stay put so their children can be lifelong friends. That's Savannah."

So much for thinking Jade wasn't liked at the party
the other night. Because she was obviously very well-
liked among *her* people, as she called them—the modern, hard-working businesspeople of a thriving
modern city. They didn't just like her. They admired
her, looked up to her. Hell, they *loved* her.

How on earth she could be the thief he knew her to
be, he had no idea. It didn't make sense. He'd thought
it over a dozen different ways since their first night together, but no matter how he looked at it, the idea of Jade
actually stealing from someone seemed impossible.

But his grandmother had told him she had. And the
painting was missing.

The frustration of not knowing what to believe was
driving him insane. He wanted to get the whole thing
out in the open and done with. Whatever kind of trouble Jade was in—whatever would lead her to such a
desperate choice—he wanted to know. To help her
solve it, and to move on.

Until she trusted him enough to open up to him,
however, he didn't think he'd be getting the answers
he wanted. Not without giving her enough reason to
disappear from his life for good. Like the fact that he'd
been lying to her from the minute they'd met.

"How's your article coming?" she asked, giving him
something else to think about.

The article. The one he was supposed to be writing
about the architecture of old Georgia. The one he hadn't
even started yet. "It's okay. Today should give me some
new angles."

"Good. You'll love the Martinique place. The man who built it back in the mid-eighteen hundreds had every stone in the garden wall brought over from the ruins of an ancient castle in France."

"Probably because his wife asked him to, huh?"

She looked disgruntled. "Now how did you know that?"

"Isn't every romantic story about walls being moved or Taj Mahals being constructed somehow related to a man totally out of his mind over a woman?"

"Pessimist."

"Romantic," he shot back.

"I don't think anyone's ever called me that before. Pragmatist, yes. Romantic, no."

"Wicked," he offered.

"Without question."

He couldn't help twining his fingers in hers and bringing her hand to his mouth for a quick kiss. "I wouldn't change a thing."

Except maybe her side job as a thief.

"Have you studied any of the guidebooks to get a history of the area?" she asked.

He nodded, but didn't elaborate on what he already knew. He wanted to see Jade's world through her eyes. She was the ultimate tour guide—a woman who could trace her ancestry right back to the slave quarters *and* the mansion of a Southern plantation. Unbelievable.

"Is the place lecherous old great-great-grandpa Lester used to own still around?"

"Four greats," she corrected. Then she shook her head. "And no, it burnt to the ground. Sherman spared much of Savannah, but not a lot outside it." She wrapped her arms around herself. "I did visit the site once. Lots of ghosts there." She didn't sound like she was being fanciful, merely introspective.

"How were you able…"

"To track down the family tree?" she asked, as if reading his mind. "I didn't have to do anything. The members of my family all like to keep records. And to talk."

"Including Lula Mae?" he asked, not letting on that he'd actually met the woman. He wasn't ready to share that tidbit with Jade yet because it would invite a discussion about why he'd been at her place.

"She's not a blood relative," she explained. "My great-grandfather married Lula Mae's mother, a Jamaican immigrant, when my grandmother was a little girl. He adopted her. The two girls were raised like sisters, which scandalized the Old Guard. It got so bad they had to leave Savannah for several years." Her voice held a tinge of hurt for her elderly relative, for the pain she'd experienced decades ago.

"But she's here now."

"Home. With her family. We love her dearly. She's been like another grandmother to Jenny and me since we were little." Then she rolled her eyes. "That voodoo stuff is highly exaggerated, but she gets a kick out of the rumors."

Their conversation was interrupted when they arrived at their destination. Ryan turned the car off the main road, following Jade's directions and some small white signs. Martinique Plantation might be a popular tourist spot, but it was well hidden behind enormous groves of pecan trees, which lined the road leading to the parking lot.

"Beautiful," he said, whistling as he looked at the facade of the building.

"Wait 'til you see the inside."

And she was right. The inside of the place was perfectly decorated and furnished, every item either unique to the period or a fine replica. Ryan hadn't been too surprised when they'd been allowed to enter the museum without an escort. The woman at the entrance had called Jade by name, chatted about the summer heat and parties and hairdos, and ushered them in without asking for the usual donation.

Though he wouldn't have believed anything could capture his interest as much as the woman at his side, he found himself getting caught up in the ambiance. Little touches of elegance and pride of workmanship shone in the mellowed oak of the floor, polished to a high sheen. Some unusual angles used in the balustrade deserved closer attention, as did the wainscoting in the dining room. The magazine planned to send a photographer to some of the buildings he mentioned in the article. The grand staircase to this place might make a nice center spread.

Strangely, when they entered what had once been a grand drawing room, he began to feel a sense of familiarity. He cast his eyes around the room, focused on nothing, but taking it all in. A large room, tastefully furnished. Groupings of red velvet sofas and cherrywood tables stood at either end. A harpsichord sat next to a set of French doors leading out to the expansive veranda.

"Come look at this," Jade said, tugging at his arm. "Here's the bride of the man who built this house. She was a renowned beauty in her time. Maybe you'll understand a little more about his grand gesture."

Then he saw it—the familiar sight that his subconscious had recognized before his eyes had even been aware of. He gaped, his jaw falling open as he beheld the painting hanging over an enormous fireplace.

The one he'd last seen on a wall at his grandparents' house in upstate New York.

RYAN SOMEHOW MANAGED to keep himself from confronting Jade about the painting right there in the drawing room of the Martinique house. It wasn't easy. He'd stood there, slack-jawed, staring at the thing, knowing for sure it was the same painting he'd gazed at so many times in his grandmother's house. Mainly because the attractive woman in it was wearing a very low-cut gown. For a twelve-year-old boy, it had been about as close to titillation as he could get in an old-people house that didn't have so much as a *National Geographic* to ogle.

He hadn't known how to react—whether to confront Jade, accuse her, try to reason with her or take the painting off the wall and run like hell. Fortunately, Jade hadn't noticed his preoccupation with the portrait. She'd bought his story that he was deep in thought about the article, when in truth he was trying to figure out what was going on.

He was still a little shell-shocked a couple of hours later, sitting alone in his hotel room. He'd made an excuse—an important interview—and driven them back to the city right after they'd finished at the first house. Jade had seemed surprised, but she hadn't objected. Only when he'd dropped her off in front of her office had he noticed her look of confusion. It had probably been matched by his own, but there hadn't been anything he could do about it.

He had to think. To be alone. To have a drink from room service.

A double.

As he sipped his gin and tonic, he tried to piece it together. Jade had stolen the painting. The painting was now in a Southern plantation house on display for everyone to see, not hidden away. He knew there was a black market for stolen art, particularly anything by the Impressionists. But he'd never have thought a legitimate museum would be involved with a shady transaction. So it was likely they hadn't known the painting was stolen when they'd purchased it from Jade.

Seeing the glaring, full-color reminder of his purpose in being here, it was impossible *not* to let the reason for his trip here interrupt the happy, lust-filled daze he'd been living in. He'd come to Savannah to track down his grandmother's property, and to get vengeance on the woman who'd stolen it.

His lover.

"What a mess," he muttered as he sat on his hotel bed, sifting through notes, maps and brochures he'd been collecting for the article. Some of the brochures were for the local homes, including Martinique Plantation.

Even here he couldn't get away from the problem. Front and center on the Martinique brochure was a color picture of the LeBeuf painting. Below it, in fancy text, was an invitation to come see the painting that had long ago been lost.

The museum was touting its return to its rightful home because it had been…"Stolen during the Civil War?"

That widened his eyes and had him reaching for his drink again. He couldn't imagine what Grandmother would think about having stolen goods in her house.

Ryan continued to read. "The piece has recently been donated by a generous and anonymous benefactor, and is on display during regular operating hours."

Donated. On display.

"Dammit, Jade, what have you been doing?"

But he knew. He didn't even have to think about it.

Jade was doing what she always did. Taking control. Righting a wrong. Getting justice, even if she had to go about it by stepping outside of the law.

She'd stolen the painting so she could return it to its original home.

Foolish. Risky. Daring. Honorable in a twisted sort of way. How like Jade.

He finally understood all the pieces that hadn't made sense—Jade's innate sense of justice, her love of history and tradition and culture. She was doing her part to set things right, in the only way she could.

The realization sent a feeling he couldn't quite define rushing through him. Relief? Gratitude?

Above all, happiness. Because while she *was* a thief, she wasn't necessarily an immoral person. She was living by her own code of right and wrong. Which was, really, all that could be expected of anyone when you came right down to it.

He'd expect nothing more from the woman he believed he was falling in love with. The one he knew he cared for more than he'd ever cared for anyone in his life.

The realization cleared things in his mind. He didn't have to feel guilty for caring for her. Jade was every bit the eccentric, dynamic, exotic, amazing woman he thought she was. And she stole stuff when she felt she had a good reason. Case closed.

So he now had only two problems to deal with. First, how to deal with his grandmother's painting.

And second, how to extricate Jade from her life of crime.

10

"I CAN'T BELIEVE YOU kidnapped me," Jade said.

Ryan ignored the disgruntled tone in Jade's voice as he drove toward Tybee Island the next afternoon. Because she wasn't disgruntled. She was just pretending to be. "When's the last time you took a vacation?"

She tapped her finger on her lips, thinking about it.

"I rest my case."

"This isn't exactly a typical vacation day. You practically carried me out of the office."

She was right, and he smiled at the memory.

Jade had at first refused to take more time off work, since she'd been out the previous day. But because one of her least reliable tour guides had come up with an excuse, she'd had to work the night tour again. She deserved the afternoon off, and he was making sure she got it. So he'd grabbed her around the waist and nearly dragged her to the door, with the aid and assistance of Daisy. After a quick trip to her house to pick up some essentials, they'd headed for Tybee Island.

"You do realize tourists are the only people crazy enough to go to the beach on a day like this."

"Why?"

She shot him a look and rolled her eyes. "It's blazing hot. Ever clued in to the whole *siesta* concept? Sleeping in the afternoon during the hottest part of the day?"

He immediately leapt on the opening. "Are you saying you want to go back to the hotel and go to bed for the afternoon?"

She chuckled. "No, you lusty man, I'm saying you're going to fry yourself like a pickle if you don't go heavy on the sunscreen."

The pickle comment probably would have elicited a reaction if he hadn't already seen the fried pickles on the menus of several local restaurants. "I already lotioned up. High SPF."

"My father used to say the same thing. And he'd fry as only an Irishman can under a Georgia summer sun." She was smiling, but he heard a wistful sound she couldn't quite hide. "I was thinking of him earlier," she added, "when you picked me up and I smelled the suntan lotion you'd put on."

"Why?"

"Coppertone. It has such a distinct smell. Makes my mind trip right back to my childhood and fills my head with warm and happy thoughts. One of those scent memory things, you know?"

He didn't follow. Obviously seeing his inquisitive look, she explained. "There are some smells that trigger memories, emotions. Haven't you ever experienced that?"

He couldn't say he had, but knew Jade was very serious about it. She appeared both lost in thought but very much aware of every word they spoke, every breath she took.

Reaching over, he dropped a hand on her leg. "No, I don't think I have."

She covered his hand with one of her own. "Have you ever lost someone, Ryan? Someone you *really* loved?"

Again he shook his head. "I've been lucky. Product of a normal childhood, all my grandparents still living, no tragedies in the Stoddard family tree."

"Ah." She nodded as if completely understanding, even though he still wasn't following her.

"Then you wouldn't get it." She reached into the back seat, retrieving a large beach bag, and pulled out a familiar brown bottle of suntan lotion. Flipping open the top with her thumb, she brought it to her nose and inhaled deeply.

He was shocked to see tears suddenly sparkling on her long lashes. She blinked rapidly. Then she held the bottle out so he could smell it.

"Smells like lotion to me."

"And to me it smells like my father." She reached up to touch the corners of her eyes and wiped away the moisture there. "You see, the innermost mind still mourns before the logical one has the chance to realize what we're grieving."

He suddenly understood and his heart broke a little for her. "I guess I do see," he admitted, lacing his fingers through hers. "Maybe that's why whenever I smell cinnamon I think of my grandmother's Christmas tree. She always hung spiced pine cones inside the branches and her whole house smelled of cinnamon every December. Someday that smell is going to give me flashes of sadness, isn't it?"

"Exactly," she said with a nod. "But happiness, too."

He pulled her fingertips to his lips and pressed a kiss to them. "I wish I'd met your dad."

She was quiet for a moment. "So do I. I think he's been on my mind so much because of you. Because of how much he would have liked you." Then she chuckled. "I've also been thinking how happy he'd be that there's apparently a little of my crazily romantic mother in me after all."

He wondered at her comment, but before he could ask about it, she continued. "By the way, for the rest of my life when I smell night-blooming jasmine with a hint of magnolia, I'll think of you. And the night we met."

So would he. He already wanted to drench himself in the scent and never let it go.

In the passenger seat, Jade stretched in the sunlight blazing through the sunroof, like a cat taking in the heat. Her whole body seemed to savor the warmth. So much for her grumbling.

"You're *glad* we're going to the beach. Admit it."

"Maybe," she said with a chuckle. "Why'd you want to do it, anyway?"

"Because I'm hot."

"That's bright," she said, a hint of dryness in her voice.

He took no offense. "At least this way I can get my whole body wet in the ocean, with very little on, instead of just getting my *clothes* wet because I'm dripping sweat in the heat and humidity."

He wasn't lying but it wasn't the only reason Ryan had suggested an afternoon at the beach. He also wanted to see the wind whip her long dark hair off her face. To watch her lick saltwater off her lips. To drown in need as he saw her hands on her skin, rubbing lotion onto her body with the unconsciously seductive movements that were second nature to her.

To talk to her, delve into her emotions and her past. Get to know her better by understanding just how deeply her feelings ran, how much sadness she'd had to deal with in her young life and what might drive her to do the things she did.

Lots of reasons.

"Pretty empty," he mumbled as he parked his rented car in a public lot near the dunes.

"Yes it is," she replied. "Like I said, only tourists come out on a day as hot as this. And usually just the British ones whose summers last two minutes."

When they got their stuff from the trunk of the car and walked down to the public beach, Ryan realized Jade was right. The place was nearly deserted. The long stretch of white sand meeting the frothy blue-green waves of the Atlantic was occupied by only a few groups of people, one with young children. It was a workday, but he'd expected at least a few more out-of-towners as crazy as himself.

"Hope they lotioned up," Jade murmured.

Choosing a spot a few yards from the water, Ryan put the cooler down and opened their two chairs while Jade spread out the rest of their gear. Kicking off his shoes, he prepared to revel in the rough sensation of sandy beach against his feet.

It felt more like burning charcoal. "Sonofa…."

"On the towel," she said quickly, pointing to a safe place to step.

"Okay, maybe this wasn't such a great idea. Should have gone closer to the water. Now we're stuck here, on Towel Island, unless we swim with our shoes on."

"It'll make running into the surf that much more exciting." She laughed softly, then pulled her sundress off, dropping it to the blanket she'd spread between their chairs.

When Ryan saw her in the hot pink bikini, he couldn't contain a soft wolf whistle. "Okay, maybe we'll stay awhile. If you run into the surf, I'll definitely withstand the burning coals and run after you."

"My hero." She lifted a pair of sunglasses to her face, staring out at the water as she slid them on. "It's beautiful."

He still hadn't taken his eyes off her. "Very."

The surf didn't pound, it merely washed up and back, and somehow it seemed Jade's body moved to its rhythm. She lowered herself to the chair, stretched out her legs, leaned back and watched the ocean. Every movement was graceful, in sync with some inner beat, as if part of her was, as always, in tune to her sultry surroundings.

She was loving it. Loving this.

"You complained, and warned me, but you like this intense heat, don't you?"

She nodded lazily. "I do like it hot."

Ditto.

"I love the sizzle on my skin," she added. "The brightness of the sky over the ocean."

Retrieving a bottle of water from the cooler, she flipped off the top and sipped it. The moisture brought a shine to her lips. Her pink tongue flicked out as she licked it away. Then she sipped again, moaned softly, and lowered the bottle.

Such a sensual woman. She nearly brought him to his knees.

He needed a cold drink. Pronto. Just watching Jade's mouth around the tip of a bottle had him thinking of all kinds of wicked things her mouth could do.

After peeling off his shirt, he dropped it on the ground, grateful for the sunscreen. The heat baked right in, bringing instant sweat which was cooled only by the light breeze blowing off the ocean.

"How do you do it?" she asked.

Looking at Jade, he found her staring up at him. Her

glasses were down on the tip of her nose and she watched his every move from above the rim.

He thought the sand was hot? Her eyes were on fire, roaming over his body as if she was seeing him bare-chested for the first time. Actually, considering their shadow-wrapped interludes of the past few nights, he supposed she was, at least in full light. "Do what?"

"How do you keep that body when you work behind a desk nine-to-five?"

He laughed softly, liking that appreciative look on her face. He understood. That pink bathing suit of hers had him thinking of nothing but getting her out of it. He'd love to take her by the hand and lead her into the water, neither of them wearing a thing. Unfortunately, with the pasty tourists a dozen yards away, he wasn't going to get his wish.

"I work out some."

"Some?"

He shrugged. "I run with my dog a few times a week."

She cocked a brow. "You have a dog?"

He nodded. "A drooling Lab I affectionately call Mutt."

"I have a cat."

"Mutt likes cats."

"For lunch?"

He shook his head and sat next to her. "He's a big goofy drooler who loves to play with anyone. People. Cats. The mouse that got into my kitchen last year."

She grinned. "Who's taking care of him?"

"He's staying with my grandparents."

He immediately stiffened as the image of his grandmother came to mind. What on earth would she think about him sitting here, engaged in casual conversation with the woman who'd stolen from her?

What *could* she think? He couldn't explain it to her, at least not until he figured out what to do about it. And he couldn't do that until he got Jade to open up to him.

He couldn't allow anything to upset this careful balance of friendship they had during the day while being passionate lovers at night.

"Can you hand me my bag?" she asked. "I need to put some lotion on before I fry."

"You must be kidding."

She tilted her head in confusion.

"This is straight date-at-the-beach stuff, Jade. You must know I'm not going to let you put on your own lotion. I'm going to insist you let me rub it on for you."

"I don't react well to orders," she murmured.

"How about to requests?" He leaned close to her chair, until their faces were a few inches apart, and they stared at one another through their dark sunglasses. "Will you *let* me put lotion on you?"

She nibbled her lip, then slowly nodded.

He gave her a kiss, licking the tiny bit of water still clinging to the corner of her mouth. Salty, sweet, hot. Jade.

Smiling in anticipation, Ryan retrieved the bottle she'd dropped beside her sundress. He poured a healthy amount of it into his hands, then knelt beside her chair.

He started at her throat. After dribbling some of the white liquid on that hollow, he gently smoothed his fingers against the skin he'd kissed so many times in the dark of night. Then he worked his way across her collarbones, using both hands until he could cup each slim shoulder. "Your skin is already so hot."

"So's the lotion," she replied.

She didn't seem to mind. In fact, her eyes were

closed, her head tipped back and her face turned toward the sun. She was savoring this. As was he.

He spread more lotion down her arms, gently turning them to protect the lighter, more vulnerable skin underneath. As he lifted one, he paused to press a hot kiss in the hollow of her elbow, then he draped her hand across his shoulder.

"Mmm," she said on a sigh.

He moved down her body. Silently counting the few adorable, tiny freckles on her chest, he licked at one, tasting the salty sheen of sweat on her body.

"That doesn't feel like lotion," she murmured.

"How about this?"

He kissed again, sucking her skin slightly, then rubbing his tongue over the spot.

"You're going to shock the British."

"They won't be the ones coming if I have my way."

She snorted a laugh at his reference to the "The British are coming." But she still didn't open her eyes.

"Get on with it, or I'm going to burn to a crisp and you won't be able to touch me without inflicting pain."

"I only want to inflict pleasure," he murmured, then returned to the task at hand.

He dispensed more lotion onto his hand, then rubbed it on her upper chest until it disappeared. He didn't trust himself to go near those perfect breasts of hers, merely sliding his hand over the curves and moving down to cup her midriff. He thoroughly coated her flat belly, and below it to the hem of her pink bikini.

"God, I have to touch you," he muttered. She didn't react, not even when he smoothed more lotion onto his fingertips then slid them below the elastic waistband of her swimsuit.

She moaned, low in her throat, not protesting as he dropped his fingers down, lower and lower.

When he reached the soft curls between her legs, her eyes flew open. "Ryan!"

"Shh," he whispered, turning slightly to shield her from view of the other people down the beach. No one was north of them. No one south would see anything except his back as he knelt beside her.

"What are you doing to me?" she asked.

"I'm giving you another scent memory. Coconut and citrus."

"Yes, you definitely are," she whispered. "I'll never be able to use this lotion again unless you're here to put it on me."

"I'm doing a good job, aren't I? Making sure you're well covered so you don't get a sunburn."

He pressed a lethargic kiss to her neck. Then he couldn't resist going further. Jade shivered when he moved his hand down, lower, seeking that hot, wet place where he so loved to lose himself.

She was drenched. Open, soft and moist against his fingers. This time he was the one to moan. "You're wet."

"You're evil," she choked out, staring straight up at the sky.

He knew why she wouldn't look at him. One look and they'd both be lost to where they were and who was nearby. She'd want his mouth, he'd need her tongue, and his hand wouldn't be contained for long by her swimsuit.

"Stop," she protested.

He chuckled. "That sounded convincing."

"Okay, don't stop." She punctuated the demand with a tilt of her hips, inviting his further exploration.

He gladly complied, sliding one finger deep into her wetness until she shuddered.

"Shh," he whispered, licking at her earlobe, rubbing his face against her silky hair. Then he kissed her, his tongue mimicking the movement of his finger, setting a quick, heady rhythm that he knew was driving her mad.

"Ryan, please," she whimpered.

He finally gave her what he knew she wanted and flicked his thumb onto that sensitive little nub of flesh that throbbed for attention.

"Yes!" Her cry wasn't too loud, but he still hoped the tourists were hard of hearing. Or that they thought seagulls' cries sounded like a woman having an orgasm.

Which, he realized when she shuddered, clenched her fists and arched her back, she was.

SOMEHOW, MAYBE BECAUSE of the heat of the sun, the sound of the surf, or the amazing afterglow of the things Ryan had made her feel with his incredible touch, Jade drifted off to sleep.

She dreamed. Short, choppy dreams full of laughter and heat, smiles and wet kisses. The warmth of someone's hand holding hers. Just that clasp of hands made her feel more happy than she'd ever felt before.

When she opened her eyes to the brilliant blue sky and a few puffy white clouds, she instinctively flexed her right hand and found it clasped with Ryan's.

He squeezed back. "I was about to wake you up to make sure you have enough sunscreen on."

She turned to face him, still slow and lethargic from her little nap, and smiled. "And if I don't, were you going to put more on for me?"

"I don't think I'm a strong enough man for that."

She took in a deep, comfortable breath, honey-sweet satisfaction oozing through her body. Letting her mind trip back to moments ago when all she could see was the sky, all she could hear was the churning of the waves and her own choppy breaths. All she could feel was *him*. "How long was I asleep?"

"Just a little while. Twenty minutes or so. But long enough that the beach traffic has thinned out a bit."

Glancing over his shoulder, she saw that the family with the young boy had gone. Nibbling her lip, she asked, "Do you think they left because of us?"

He shook his head. "I think it had something to do with the kid lying about putting on some sunscreen. His mother was screeching something about him being red as a lobster as she dragged him up the beach."

"Thank goodness," she replied with a chuckle. Then she rose from the chair and extended her hand. "Let's go for a swim."

"I thought you'd never ask."

They dropped their sunglasses onto their chairs then dashed, hand in hand, into the surf. The shock of cold water against her ankles made Jade moan in appreciation. Her whole body was sticky hot, and the cool waters of the Atlantic provided exactly the relief she needed.

They dove under the next wave, rising a few yards out beyond the break.

"Have I thanked you yet for suggesting this?" she asked as they treaded water.

"Not with words."

"Thanks," she replied. Then she gave him a saucy grin. "With words."

"Have I thanked you, yet, for tying me up naked to a statue in Mamie Brandywine's garden?"

She laughed aloud. "Not with words."

He swam closer, shaking water off his hair as he pulled her into his arms. "Thanks, Jade. I'm beginning to think this trip to Savannah might be one of the best things I ever did."

She studied his face, gauging his meaning. His voice had sounded husky, but also sincere. He stared back at her, as if not seeing the sopping hair and sun-reddened face. His expression said a lot about what he was thinking, what he was feeling.

The same things she was?

Whatever crazy feelings were swirling around here about this—this *thing* they'd fallen into—she wasn't the only one feeling them.

A wave washed over them, pushing them closer to shore until they could stand chest-deep in the water. Ryan slid his arms around her shoulders and pulled her close. "No children or harried moms to be shocked if we kiss."

She snorted a laugh. "I think we did a little more than kiss on the beach."

Instead of replying, he lowered his mouth to hers, sweeping his tongue along her lips. Salty. Minty. Delicious.

She kissed him back and tilted against him, sliding her wet body against his beneath the surface of the water.

He groaned against her lips. She knew why when she felt his instant reaction. "It's pretty deserted," she said. Her voice was low, wicked.

"You're so bad."

"Isn't that why you like me?"

He nodded. "One of many reasons."

One of many. That implied he liked her a lot, didn't

it? Darn good thing. Because she suspected she more than liked this man. Amazing, really. Someone she'd set out to destroy might turn out to be the man she'd been waiting for all her life.

"So what are you suggesting?" he asked, slipping his hands down to cup her waist, then her hips. Then lower, until he was playing with the waistband of her bottoms.

"What do you think I was suggesting?" She wrapped one leg around him, curving herself more intimately against him until he sucked in a harsh breath.

"I don't exactly have condoms in the pocket of my trunks."

"Shucks." She rubbed against him again, drawing out the torture for both of them.

"I'm not going to be able to walk out of the water for a good ten minutes now."

She glanced toward the beach. Now, with the full afternoon heat blazing down, more people had left to escape the sun. "Unless those two guys fishing down there have a pair of binoculars, they're not going to have any idea what we're doing under the waves."

"I like how you think."

"You're gonna like my next move even better," she promised. Without warning, she reached into the waistband of his trunks and captured his thick, throbbing erection in her hand.

"Oh, yeah," he managed to croak out between ragged breaths. "I definitely like that."

She liked it, too. Liked the solid, heavy weight of him in her palm. Liked how he moaned when she squeezed. Liked feeling so wicked and wanton and elemental with the roll of the waves and the far-off cry of seagulls in the background.

"If a wave comes and knocks us down, I'm gonna end up bare-ass naked on the beach with my trunks around my knees," he said, weakly trying to protest. She knew he didn't want her to stop. The way his head was thrown back and his lips parted told her he loved what she was doing. Each stroke brought another slight groan. Each roll of her thumb over the tip of his erection made him shake.

"Do you really care?" She rose on tiptoe to press a kiss against the base of his throat, the taste of salt water mixed with the salty essence of man completely intoxicating her.

He could only shake his head, then lower his mouth to hers to grab a deep, wet kiss even as he grabbed another deep breath. Without a single protest, he gave himself over to Jade as she took him to the same heights of pleasure where he'd so recently taken her.

By the time they came out of the water, he could only think that he was damned glad he'd used the waterproof sunscreen.

11

A FEW NIGHTS LATER, Ryan was ready to confront Jade about her secret life of crime and offer to help her work through it. Because he'd come to a few conclusions.

First, he couldn't keep up the deception. He hated lying, *hated* it. And lying to someone he cared about was proving too much to bear.

Second, until he figured out how to extract Jade from the sticky legal situation she'd gotten herself into, he wouldn't feel safe loving her.

Loving her. God, that sounded dramatic. He'd known the woman only slightly more than a week and he'd fallen in love with her.

Well, why not? He'd been engaged to a woman for a year and had never felt one moment of the pure joy he shared with Jade.

Besides, he'd simply followed in the footsteps of his family, hadn't he? His grandparents, parents and sister—they'd all met their one-and-only, their soul mate—and had never been willing to settle for anything else.

His grandmother had been warning him for years that he came from passionate stock. That when the right woman came along, he'd know, down to his bones, that she was the one person in the world he couldn't do without.

"What you t'inking, boy?"

Ryan looked up from the fabulous fried-chicken-and-okra dinner Aunt Lula Mae had made for them tonight and caught the old woman watching him with a knowing smile. Jade had invited him over to meet her much-loved relative. Neither Ryan nor Lula Mae had admitted that they'd already met. Lula Mae seemed to enjoy conspiracy—she'd given him several broad smiles and surreptitious winks throughout the evening.

"You know what I'm thinking about," he replied, knowing he was right. Whether she was truly into anything supernatural, the old woman had an uncanny ability to read people.

"You wonderin' how Jade gonna react when she fin' out you came here 'dat night. Because you don' trust her."

He glanced around the sparse dining room, furnished only with a small table and four chairs, to make sure Jade hadn't returned from her bedroom, where she'd gone to take a call during their dinner.

"*Didn't*," he clarified. "I understand her much better now."

Lula Mae nodded, setting the thick strand of beads around her neck clicking against her throat. No bunny slippers tonight. No chicken claws, either. She was dressed in a brightly-colored, loose dress with an island pattern. A red bandanna covered her spiky gray hair, and on her fingers she wore a number of large rings. She pointed one of those ringed fingers in his direction. "You see? You understan' the truth now?"

He nodded. "Jade doesn't think she's doing anything wrong."

Lula Mae nodded. "She never do anything she know is wrong."

"But she could get herself into trouble."

The woman cackled. "Didn't she already, when she hook up wid' you?"

Trouble? Maybe at first. But not now. Having spent nearly every hour in each other's company for the past several days, troublesome was not how he'd describe their relationship.

Exciting. Passionate. Playful. Sultry. Oh, yes, all those things. Things he'd almost forgotten he wanted and now knew he couldn't do without. Just like he couldn't do without her.

His grandmother, as it turned out, was right.

"I'm supposed to go back to New York tomorrow," he told Lula Mae, letting her hear his genuine anxiety.

He hated to make that trip for another reason as well. Because he'd have to go face Grandmother and tell her that if she wanted her stolen painting back, she was going to have to fight the Savannah Historical Society. Not to mention one more little tidbit—that if he had his way, she was going to be setting one more place at the table come Thanksgiving.

For Jade, the con woman his grandmother had sent him to find. The woman he planned to spend the rest of his rich, exciting, passionate life with.

How did I ever get by without her.

He didn't voice his question aloud, but Lula Mae seemed to know to answer, anyway. "Jade, she's like you. Not bein' true to herself, not lettin' anyone too close because she feel she got to protect all of us. Now, though, she doesn't have her mama and Jenny to play mama to. So time for her to have a life of her own."

With you.

This time, he was the one who heard the words the old woman didn't say.

"Well, it sounds like we met each other at exactly the perfect time in both our lives, doesn't it?"

He didn't even realize Jade had entered the room until she answered. "Absolutely."

She greeted him with the kind of open, genuine smile that made him shake under its power. Jade when sultry and wicked was deadly. Jade when happy and sunny was simply beyond resisting.

And he had no intention whatsoever of doing that.

"Lula Mae, if I could ever get my grandmother to visit Savannah, I want you to cook these greens for her."

The woman waved off his compliment with an airy hand.

"Speaking of which," he said, turning his attention to Jade, who'd settled back in her seat, "I have to go home tomorrow. Got to get back to work, pull an article out of my Jade-fried brain and meet my deadline."

"Wonderful," she replied, not looking at all dismayed by the prospect of him leaving.

Her response was deflating, to say the least. Then he saw the grin on her lips and knew she was toying with him.

"Because," she continued, "it just so happens that I need to make a trip up to New York, as well."

"Really?"

She nodded, then nibbled delicately at a piece of chicken. She remained silent, licking her lips and tasting the meat. She shot a look at Lula Mae. "You used something different in this."

The old woman merely smiled and shrugged before getting up to clear the table. "What fun is spice if you can't play with it?"

"She's always trying out different things," Jade said

once the older woman had left the room. "I'm some-times afraid to ask where she gets this stuff."

"As long as it doesn't come from midnight flowers blooming on a grave on a moonless night, I have to say I approve of her cooking."

"I think midnight flowers only bloom in graveyards when there's a full moon."

"The better for the werewolves?"

She tsked. "There's nothing as gauche as were-wolves in Savannah. Maybe vampires." She gave him a heated look, telling him where her thoughts had gone. "Have I ever told you about my vampire fan-tasies?"

He shook his head. "No, but I think I'd like to hear about them."

"I think you'd love to hear about them," she retorted with a definite lick of her lips.

He shifted in his seat, trying to remember that Lula Mae was in the next room. "I don't remember hearing you mention vampires on any of your tours."

She shrugged. "I don't. Only ghosts. Weren't you paying attention?"

He'd gone on three of Jade's tours now and learned as much as he wanted to about the ghosts who popu-lated the most haunted city in the U.S. "Yes, I was pay-ing attention. But today I kept getting distracted by the wiggle of the woman walking in front of me during the tour."

She shot him a glare. "That blonde had a lot of wig-gle in her walk."

"She had a lot of wiggle in a good stiff breeze," Ryan replied, sparing barely a thought for the bimbo who'd made a play for him today right in front of Jade.

Jade hadn't so much as batted an eyelash. But she'd

gotten her revenge, telling a particularly gruesome story about the murder of a blond tart who preyed on other women's men back in the twenties. Ryan hadn't known whether to feel sorry for the woman, who'd blanched red, or laugh his head off at Jade for being jealous.

Leaning across the cluttered table, he pressed a kiss on her shiny lips. "I was talking about my tour guide. The woman who's taught me quite a lot this past week."

"Like, not to go to the beach in the middle of a July afternoon unless you want to become as crispy as this chicken?"

He snorted. "Are you kidding? That was the best trip to the beach I ever had! I'll never want to go in the ocean again if you're not with me."

"I think you mean *come* in the ocean," she replied, completely deadpan.

He barked a laugh. "Oh, did I ever set myself up for that." He pulled Jade from her chair and onto his own lap. "You are so bad."

"And so are you," she replied, pressing a kiss against his lips before tucking her head against his neck. "Thank goodness."

He liked holding her. Liked feeling her in his lap, curled up in complete trust and comfort.

"Now, tell me why you're coming to New York. When we can leave. How long you can stay. And promise you'll wait outside my apartment door for ten minutes when we get there so I can change the sheets, hide my stash of porn, and make sure the toilet seat's down."

He should have known she wouldn't focus on the sheets.

"Porn?"

"I was a bachelor in my former life."

"A naughty one."

"Why do you think we go together so well?"

"Like Bonnie and Clyde."

Whoa, that comparison cut a little too close for comfort. But it was a perfect opening. "Jade—"

Lula Mae came back into the dining room before he could open up the conversation about Jade's secret life as a stolen-art avenger.

Hmm…sounded like the name of a dark superheroine. He could totally get into seeing Jade in a skintight spandex catsuit. He closed his eyes to appreciate the mental flash.

"Aunt Lula Mae, do you think you'd mind going and staying with Tally for a couple of days?" Jade asked.

The woman pursed her lips. "She doesn't have HBO. I don' wanna miss any *Sex and the City* reruns."

"You've seen every episode. And Mama has the first season on tape anyway. We can pick them up from her place if you can't survive without them," Jade said with a roll of her eyes.

"You don' have to go out of state if you want to fool around with your man," Lula Mae said with a wag of her thin, gray eyebrows. "I got bad hearing."

"You hear like a guard dog," Jade retorted.

Lula Mae smirked.

"And I'm not going for that reason," Jade added as she rose from Ryan's lap to stand beside the table. "I just confirmed a meeting with someone who has something I've been looking for."

Ryan immediately went on alert. "What do you mean?"

Jade shrugged but didn't meet his eyes. "I've been investigating the disappearance of a famous pair of dueling flintlocks from the Harrison estate."

Oh, no. Dueling pistols. Sounded old, antique, Civil War–era.

"What does it have to do with you?" he asked, meeting Lula Mae's speculative stare over Jade's shoulder.

Jade busied herself by picking up the remaining dishes from the table. "It's a sideline. I like going on treasure hunts for the Historical Society. I'm going to visit the current owner, who happens to live up in New York. Seems like a whole regiment of New Yorkers spent some time in Savannah during the war."

Visit. Would she pose as a gun appraiser this time? A historian? A potential buyer? Or would she don all-black and creep into a strange house late at night to steal back what somebody stole more than a century ago? "Jade, you don't mean to—"

"Okay," Lula Mae interrupted. "I'll stay with Tally. And I bring Jinx, too."

Jade paused, dirty dishes in hand. "Tally hates cats. I can ask the neighbor to look in on him."

Lula Mae merely shrugged. "Jinx don't go, I don't go."

Jade groaned and glanced at Ryan. "She likes to scare Tally's housemaid. Voodoo priestess, black cat and all that stuff. She's as big an actress as Jenny." Then she sighed. "And Mama."

The old woman continued as if Jade hadn't spoken. "You go have fun on one of your treasure hunts." Turning to Ryan, she shook her finger at him. "And you make sure you stay close to keep my girl out of trouble."

"Trouble? Now why would I possibly get in any trouble?"

Ryan could think of a bunch of reasons—police, criminal charges and armed homeowners among them.

Lula Mae shot him another warning look. She seemed to be telling Ryan not to confront Jade about what she was doing. He wanted to, more than anything. He wanted to get things out in the open and do whatever he had to—including locking Jade in her room, if that's what it took—to get her to give up this crazy idea.

Again, though, when he opened his mouth, Lula Mae pointed an index finger at him and shook her head.

Maybe the old woman was right. Jade cared about him. He *knew* she did. He'd even go so far as to say he believed she was falling in love with him, as he was with her.

But she'd only known him a little over a week. She didn't entirely trust him yet, as evidenced by the way she was so evasive about her "treasure hunt." She'd already proven she was a woman who didn't like being told what to do. If he confronted her and demanded that she give up this crazy Robin Hood lifestyle of hers, she might become furious and have the opposite reaction.

She could run from him, from *them*, and get herself into even more trouble.

Which meant there was only one thing he could do. Stick to her like glue and save Jade from herself.

JADE LIKED NEW YORK. Even though her heart belonged in the South, she could appreciate the big thriving city that pulsed with life and excitement. What wasn't to love about a place that could turn its seediest areas into major tourist attractions? Savannah with its River

Walk. New Orleans with Bourbon Street. And New York City with Times Square.

They'd all adopted a take-charge attitude to overcome the past. They'd charged freely into the future, making a delight out of what had once been looked down upon. Kind of reminded her of some people she knew. Like herself.

Ryan was an incredibly attentive host. He rarely left her side the first two days, insisting he could do his work from home. He also wanted to accompany her wherever she went.

Funny, it was as if he was really afraid to leave her alone. She found herself touched by the protectiveness, since Jade had pretty much looked after herself from the time she was a kid. But she wasn't used to it, and finally told him one morning that she was going to meet her sister for breakfast, *alone*, whether he liked it or not.

"I don't like it," he grumbled as he leaned against his dresser, arms crossed in front of his chest.

She didn't look away from the mirror as she calmly continued to apply her makeup. "But—"

"But I know you have to leave and you're a big girl and you won't get lost and the Big Bad Wolf isn't going to gobble you up while you're walking down Fifth Avenue," he admitted.

"Correct," she replied after he rattled off the arguments she'd used with him moments before. "Now, I still haven't gotten a call back from Richard Brewer, the man I've been trying to see. I thought I'd have heard from him by now. Please take a message if he calls, okay?"

He merely shrugged, then got back to her day-trip. "You're just going for breakfast, right? You should take cabs there and right back so you don't get lost. This is a big city."

She slid some mascara over her lashes. "I've been in big cities before."

"You'll go straight to the restaurant and straight back?"

She closed the tube of mascara and rolled her eyes. "You bet." She finished up her lipstick, ran the brush through her hair one more time, then grabbed her purse. "Now, Mr. Overprotective, may I please go have breakfast with my sister?"

He lowered his eyes. "I'm being a caveman, huh?"

"Nah. Just a worrier."

He put his hands on her shoulders, holding her still so he could stare into her face. "I don't want anything happening to you. I don't want you to get into any trouble."

She quirked a brow. "Spoken like a man who stripped naked in a garden for a complete stranger just a couple of weeks ago."

"I think you hexed me," he replied. "Used some of Lula Mae's juju on me."

"You've been reading The Book again, haven't you?"

"Nope. Just wondering how on earth I left this apartment two weeks ago convinced I'd be a bachelor for a long, long time, and now I can't picture my world without you in it."

Jade froze, waiting for a funny remark, an offhand wink or something that would indicate Ryan was just playing around. He didn't laugh, didn't wink, didn't lighten the moment in any way. He merely stared at her with an intense, honest gaze that made his green eyes shine even brighter and made her heart thud in her chest.

Didn't most people think it took *time* to fall in love, time to decide when you'd found the person you wanted to spend your life with? Jade knew better. She was a Dupré, after all. The tendency to love fast and love hard was in her blood.

Fortunately, she was also a Maguire. Which meant she was like her father—emotional, deeply loyal, a believer in loving with her whole heart and holding back nothing. The kind of person who'd love only once. For a lifetime.

She also knew now that she was in love with Ryan Stoddard. She just hadn't been ready to admit it, nor did she think he was ready to hear it, much less that he was feeling the same way.

So his words came as something of a shock. "Ryan—"

"Come back soon, Jade," he said, pressing a kiss to her forehead, as if he recognized the door he'd opened with his words. "Promise."

Okay, he wasn't ready to talk. Neither was she, really. But just the things they'd hinted at had filled her mind with the most wonderful visions of a future for them, something she hadn't really dared think about before.

Giving him a soft kiss on the lips, she nodded. "I will."

Leaving his plush building, complete with uniformed doorman, Jade thought again about Ryan's background. They'd never talked about it, but there was no question the man had money. That could be an obstacle.

So could geography. Jade liked New York, but she didn't want to live here. She hated the thought of leaving Savannah.

"He's worth it," she whispered, drawing a stare from someone walking past her on the sidewalk.

The stranger, a young woman carrying a ton of shopping bags, paused, then gave her a broad, New York smile. "If he puts that look on your face, lady, he's definitely worth it!"

Good lord, even strangers were commenting on her love life. But she couldn't help smiling back.

When she reached the restaurant where Jenny worked, she sat in a booth and waited for her sister to show up. She didn't know why Jenny wanted to meet *here*. Jade would have figured she'd want to stay as far away as possible from her place of employment on her day off. But there was no second-guessing Jenny's motives about anything.

"You really are here!" her sister said when she arrived, bending down and giving Jade a kiss on the cheek. "I hadn't expected to see you for months. I'm so excited. But why aren't you staying with me? How long will you be in town?"

As usual, Jade found it hard to get a word in edgewise. When Jenny stopped for breath, Jade said, "Nice to see you, too. I'm here on business. I don't know how long I'll be around. And we have to talk."

Jenny's pretty face immediately pulled into the pretty pout that had always helped her get her way. "Am I in trouble?"

"That depends on your definition of trouble," Jade said dryly. "But you're certainly high on my shit-list right now."

Jenny's brows shot up. Jade had been mothering her sister for so long, she couldn't remember the last time they'd really argued. Jenny was probably also shocked that Jade had actually used a swear word—in public, no less. Jade had played the responsible one for so long, she'd seldom voiced her true feelings and emotions out loud.

Not until Ryan, anyway.

The last time she'd really erupted at her sister was probably when Jenny had decided to move to New York without a job or more than a hundred bucks. And Jade had informed her she was "out of her effing mind."

Jade had to hand it to her. Jenny wasn't starving. In fact, she looked just beautiful. Now, if only she'd grow up emotionally…

"Why are you mad at me?" Jenny asked, leaning close as if afraid to be overheard.

Jade quickly confronted her about the Ryan situation.

"I already told you on the phone I might have exaggerated."

"Might?"

Jenny rolled her eyes. "Okay, I did. Big deal. He was hot and I was ticked off that he never asked me out. Just that lunch, which was more like an interrogation anyway."

Confused, Jade said, "What do you mean?"

"I don't know. He just asked a lot of questions about where I was from and what I did for a living, when what I really wanted him to ask was how soon I could get naked with him."

"That's my prerogative," Jade said, her jaw tight.

Jenny didn't say anything for a minute. Then her mouth fell open. "Holy crap, is that why you're asking all these questions? Are *you* involved with him?"

All around them were chattering people ordering their omelets over the din of clanking dishes, and some guy was up on stage massacring a song from *Phantom of the Opera*. Jade still shot her sister a look that said "shut up" before replying. "I am. And I wanted to let you know it, face-to-face, just in case you have any left-over feelings or problems with it."

Jenny merely smiled. "No problem. He's too old for me anyway. And I'm infatuated with this new dancer at the studio. Man, if only he weren't gay."

"Oh, boy, that's a tough road to go down."

Jenny reached across the table and grabbed Jade's hand, squeezing it tightly. "I'm so happy for you. It's about time. If Ryan is what put this…this…glow around you, then I'll love him for always."

Jade quirked a brow.

"As a brother," Jenny said with a cheeky grin.

They clinked their coffee mugs together, then Jenny instantly hit Jade with a barrage of questions. Jade updated her on Lula Mae, and on their mother—whom they'd only heard from once since she'd left on her three-week honeymoon cruise in the Mediterranean. Fortunately, when Jenny zeroed in on Jade's relationship with Ryan, demanding details on how and where they'd met, Jade was literally saved by the bell—her phone.

"Sorry, I forgot to turn it off," she said, hating people who had loud cell phone conversations in public places. She planned to ignore it, at least until she saw the name of the person calling her. "Oh, no, do you mind? I've been trying to set up a meeting with this man. He e-mailed and said I could come one day this week, but I've never gotten a phone call confirming."

Jenny waved her off, probably completely oblivious to the rudeness Jade was trying so hard to avoid. Her little sister was completely occupied with picking the mushrooms out of her omelet. Same old Jenny— liked the flavor, not the texture, so she always ordered the things, then picked them out of whatever she was eating.

Jade had a quick conversation with Mr. Brewer, the man who now owned the famous Harrison dueling pistols. She'd been investigating the disappearance of the flintlocks for a long time, using her Internet resources to track them down. She'd expected it to be tough. Paintings were so much easier. But this particular set was so distinctive it had been mentioned in an old Savannah newspaper article as the finest pair of pistols in the state of Georgia. With the accompanying description, it hadn't been too tough to find Mr. Brewer through the gun collectors' circuit.

Jade had sent the gentleman a copy of the article, not to mention a lot of other background information, right down to the manufacturer of the pistols. So Brewer probably had a darn good idea why Jade wanted to see him.

Things would go one of two ways. Either he'd listen with interest, tell her it wasn't his problem that he had something that had been stolen a century and a half ago, and invite her out. There wasn't much the Historical Society could do in that case, and most people knew it.

Or, he could be like the nice old lady in upstate New York who'd returned the Impressionist painting just last month. He might immediately donate the stolen item, trying to right an injustice of the past.

She wondered which this Mr. Brewer would do. Thankfully, she wouldn't have to wonder for long. The man lived not too far from Ryan's place, and he was open to a visit that very morning.

Though she'd promised Ryan she'd only go out for breakfast, she had time for a quick detour. Besides, once she got this business taken care of, she'd feel much more comfortable settling in for a few days' *vacation*.

Then, if she had her way, they'd never leave Ryan's apartment—or his bedroom—during the little time they had left. And maybe they'd get around to finishing that conversation they'd started this morning.

12

RYAN DIDN'T REALLY START TO worry until three hours after Jade's departure. Though he hadn't liked her going, he'd known she wanted to see her sister and hadn't been able to come up with a single good reason why she shouldn't.

He could have told her it was because he was afraid she'd make a side trip to steal, but didn't think she'd like that too much.

Until Jade confronted her sister over her lies about him, he certainly couldn't go with her. So he'd finally had to back down.

"They're just talking," he told himself. Given his firsthand knowledge of Jenny's gabbiness—which had driven him nuts from the moment they'd met—he'd expected Jade to be gone a while. But not *this* long.

Staring at the clock again, he smothered a groan. How could he focus on the article, which he was writing on the computer in his spare room? Or deal with the ton of e-mail, or check up on his day job? He couldn't keep his attention on *any* of it until he knew for sure Jade was okay—not in jail, or facing the end of an angry gun collector's pistol.

He shouldn't have let her leave. Lula Mae had warned him, plus his own instincts had been screaming at him. Not just to keep her in sight, but to confront her and get this business out in the open once and for all. But he'd hesitated, for what he now recognized were primarily selfish reasons.

Fact was, he didn't want to risk losing her. Didn't want to upset the tenuous balance of their new relationship. Didn't want her to walk out of here with a look of disgust on her face when she found out he was a liar.

Didn't want her to see a trace of dismay on his own face when she admitted she was a thief.

"Damn," he muttered, getting up again and prowling around his apartment.

It was while on the prowl that he thought to pick up the phone and call her on her cell. The double-fast dial tone told him he had a message.

Uh-oh.

Calling in to check the message, he cursed the twenty minutes he'd taken to grab a shower because during that time, two calls had come in. The first from Jade's potential victim, Mr. Brewer. He'd left a number, then said he would try to reach Jade on her cell phone.

"Oh, great."

The second call had come ten minutes later. From Jade.

"No, no, no," he muttered aloud as he listened to her soft voice with that underlying hint of Southern smoothness she hadn't completely eradicated. Brewer had tracked her down. She was going to see him.

After slamming down the phone, Ryan ran a frustrated hand through his hair. "She promised!"

In her message, she'd apologized for breaking that promise, tempting him by saying she wanted to get her business out of the way so she could devote every minute of the next few days to him. To *them.*

Unfortunately, there wouldn't be a next few days if she wound up in jail. Or hurt.

Thinking quickly, Ryan hurried into his office and pulled up a familiar Web site on his computer. Doing a reverse check on the phone number, he found the address for a Mr. Richard Brewer. Not believing his good luck, he realized the man lived only a short cab ride away.

Without giving it another thought, he left his apartment. Jade's days as a thief were over, starting now. Even if he had to steal the stupid guns back from her and return them to their owner, he was going to end this dangerous game she was playing.

Then he was going to see to it she was much too busy to play games with anybody but him.

MR. BREWER WAS A frail-looking old man, but he had a sharp-eyed stare that belied his slow movements. Jade sensed he'd been a business shark in his younger days. A widower, he lived in an apartment overlooking Central Park, so he'd likely been a *successful* shark. She figured he could afford to part with the flintlocks, at least financially.

When Jade had arrived, he'd played gracious host, serving her some iced tea before inviting her to join him in his beautifully decorated living room. He'd then spoken at length about his ancestor, an honored colonel in the Union army. His every word reinforced Jade's certainty that he did not even want to *consider* the idea that the flintlocks had been stolen.

But to Jade's surprise, he didn't seem perturbed at the idea of parting with them. He seemed more upset by the idea that his great-great-great-uncle might have looted them from a house in Savannah.

She had to tread very carefully.

"Well, of course, we have no way of knowing how

they came into the possession of Colonel Samuels, your ancestor. Perhaps he won them in a game of cards, or took them as payment from another Union officer who was responsible for the original theft."

That appeared to mollify him a bit.

"Perhaps. Do you have any children, Ms. Maguire?"

She shook her head. "No. I hope to, someday."

Then she thought of one more thing she and Ryan needed to discuss *someday*.

"My grandchildren come to visit all the time," he said as he freshened her tea. "My daughter hates guns, doesn't want her kids anywhere near them."

"Understandable," she said, bringing the glass to her lips. Horrid stuff, made with nasty-tasting powder. Then again, even freshly brewed tea tasted bad to Jade if it came from anywhere north of the Mason-Dixon line.

Mr. Brewer sat across from her, fixing his blue-eyed stare on her face. "I was thinking of *selling* the things. That's why I contacted an antique gun association to try to get more information on their worth."

Jade groaned inwardly. He'd been researching the value of the pistols. No way would she be able to offer him the kind of dollar figure they'd command at auction or private sale. Heck, she couldn't offer him *any* money at all.

The work she did on behalf of the Historical Society was on a donation or loan basis only. The society didn't have the money to purchase artifacts. Even if they could prove the items had once been stolen, the present-day descendents of the former owners usually couldn't afford the legal fees to pursue a lawsuit whose outcome was tenuous at best. If they could even be found.

Which was why Jade was so dedicated to what she did. She'd managed to talk a lot of people into donating a lot of items over the past few years. She could usually tell how things were going to progress as soon as she met the current owners, but this man had her stymied. She wasn't sure whether this was going to be a good day or a bad one.

"That is how I found you," Jade finally admitted. "Someone forwarded your posting from an antique gun Web site message board, and I began to do the research."

"Interesting line of work you're in, young lady," the old man said as he set his glass on a nearby coffee table.

"Not my line of work, exactly," she explained. "I'm a volunteer."

That seemed to surprise him. "You mean, you don't work for the Society?"

She shook her head and grinned. "I own a haunted sites tour company in Savannah. I just do this for fun."

He barked a laugh. "Some idea of fun."

The exchange seemed to have intrigued him, and he finally smiled. "All right, so tell me more about this Harrison estate. The family." Then he winked. "And the tax benefits of making such a valuable donation."

But before Jade could say another word, they were interrupted by a knock on the door to the apartment. Jade cursed the luck. She'd just about had Mr. Brewer in the right frame of mind to give away something he could sell for tens of thousands of dollars. Now, however, he was thoroughly distracted by the imperious knocking.

"One moment, young lady," the old man said as he rose from his seat. Using his cane, he carefully made his way to the entrance of the apartment. He peeked through the peephole, then opened the door only as far as the chain-lock would allow. "What do you want?"

"I'm sorry to bother you. I'm looking for someone. Miss Maguire."

That was Ryan's voice. Jade immediately rose to her feet, wondering what on earth he was doing here.

Mr. Brewer raised a curious brow, and Jade could only shrug in apology. Appearing satisfied, the old man unlocked the door and ushered Ryan inside. "Do I know you?"

Ryan strode toward the living room, answering over his shoulder. "No, sir, you don't. I'm sorry to intrude, but I have to take Miss Maguire out of here. Right now."

Her first thought was of bad news. An accident. "Something's wrong. Is it Jenny? Aunt Lula Mae?" she asked, her heart somewhere in the vicinity of her throat.

He sucked in a breath, instantly looking contrite. "No, darlin', nothing like that. But you, uh…you need to come with me. Right now." He lowered his voice and leaned closer. "Before this goes any further."

She whispered back. "Before what goes any further?"

"Yes, before what?" Mr. Brewer asked, banging his cane on the floor.

Ryan squared his shoulders. Even from a few feet away, Jade could see the pulse ticking in his jaw and the flush in his cheeks. No question something had happened. He looked more upset than he had since the night they'd met. "Sir, I'm sorry we've intruded on you. Miss Maguire and I are leaving now."

Jade's jaw fell open. From Mr. Overprotective to Mr. Freaking Neanderthal. She barely recognized this man as the flirtatious charmer she'd met at Mamie Brandywine's party.

She shook off his hand when he tried to take her arm. "Ryan, you're being ridiculous. I told you I had business to take care of."

"Not *this* kind of business," he bit out. Then he looked over his shoulder at Mr. Brewer. "Could you possibly give us a moment of privacy?"

The old man looked them both over, faint amusement evident on his face. He obviously thought they were having a lovers' quarrel.

He wasn't quite right. They were about to have a lovers' World War III if Ryan Stoddard didn't come up with a good explanation pretty darn quick.

As soon as Mr. Brewer had left them alone in the room, Jade threw Ryan's hand off her arm and put her fisted hands on her hips. "What do you think you're doing? I almost had him convinced to let me walk out of here with those flintlocks."

He took her by the upper arms and pulled her close. She felt the anger in his touch and saw the grimness of his tightly held lips. "I can't let you do it, Jade. I know you think you're doing something noble, but it's still wrong. I can't let you steal from that old man."

Steal. Steal? Had he just said *steal*?

This time her mouth didn't just open, she really thought for sure she'd heard the thud of her jaw hitting her own chest. "What are you talking about?" she managed to choke out.

"I know the truth," he said between clenched teeth. "I know you think you're being some kind of Robin Hood, stealing back stuff that was stolen and donating it to the Historical Society."

"I am *what*?"

He lowered his eyes, not meeting hers for a moment. Jade was still trying to take it all in.

Then he looked up, almost pleading with her. "You can't do it anymore. It's too dangerous and I won't let you risk it."

Wouldn't let her risk it…risk being a thief? That's what he thought she was doing here? A half-hysterical laugh, completely devoid of humor, escaped her lips. "This is crazy."

"Yeah, it is," he muttered, running a hand through his hair in frustration until it stuck up in all directions.

Her first impulse was to reach up and smooth it out. She squashed the urge. She'd be better off sticking her own fingers into a lit fire right at this moment. She suspected it might be less painful in the long run.

"I know you come from a crazy background," he added, "and that somehow you made it seem right in your mind. But you're playing a risky game, Jade, and your luck's not going to hold out. I can't stand by and watch you get caught."

"Caught," she murmured.

Heaven help her, she'd already been caught, hadn't she? Caught in a spell of love with a man who didn't know her at all. He'd nearly proclaimed his love for her a few hours ago. And now he was telling her he cared about her too much to let her get into trouble because of her *thieving*.

If he thought that…well, he didn't know her at all. She was a complete stranger to him. She had to be if he could think she was some kind of thief or con artist who'd steal from an old man because of some misplaced notions of Southern patriotism. Jade didn't know whether to laugh, cry or just pummel the distrusting louse.

The lousy man she loved.

"Wait a minute," she said, trying to put the pieces

together. "Is that why you went out with Jenny? She said you'd asked a bunch of questions." Then another thought struck. "Oh, God, that's why you came to Savannah, isn't it? You weren't there by chance—you were tracking me!"

It sounded ridiculous, but she knew by the look on his face that she'd scored a hit.

"I came after you to find something you took from someone I know," he explained tightly.

She shook her head, blinking rapidly to clear her eyes of gathering tears. "So it was all a lie. You pursued me on purpose, lying to me the whole time."

He fidgeted, then fired back. "You pursued me, too. I wasn't the one who tied you up naked to a statue in Mamie Brandywine's garden."

From the other room they heard a curious choking sound. Jade spared a second of concern for Mr. Brewer, but no more. She was too focused on what Ryan was admitting. "I already told you why I did that, because of Jenny. Which might have been the perfect time for you to admit the truth yourself."

He grabbed her hand. "I wish I had, Jade." He didn't elaborate. And frankly, she didn't really give a damn at this point.

"Tell me one thing," she finally said.

He waited.

She urged her voice to remain steady, not to crack as she voiced what might be the most important question she'd ever asked. "Tell me, knowing me as you do, do you really think I'm a thief?"

He met her stare and she silently pleaded with him to admit he was wrong. That there had been some colossal mistake, and he knew darn well she'd never be so dishonorable, so deceitful.

Instead, he just looked at her, his mouth opening, closing. But no words came out.

Without another word, she dropped his hand and walked out of the apartment.

"WELL, YOU CERTAINLY mucked that one up, didn't you, young man?"

Ryan had barely even remembered where he was—in a complete stranger's home—once Jade had stormed out. He'd been frozen, torn between what he knew to be true—based on his grandmother's words—and the look of absolute betrayal in Jade's eyes.

His head was spinning as he wondered what he'd just done.

"What did you say?" he finally asked the old man as he shook his head, trying to regain his equilibrium.

"Had the girl by the heart, and you chucked her away," Mr. Brewer said, shaking his head in disgust. "Youth is wasted on the stupid and insensitive."

He could only watch, slack-jawed, as the old gentleman sat down in a chair, pulling a wooden case onto his lap. He opened it, glanced at the items inside, then snapped it closed. "You'll take these with you and get them to her, won't you?"

Ryan stared, noting the emblem burned into the wood. "The pistols?"

"Of course the pistols," the man said with an irritated look. "Was about to give them to her when you busted in."

Ryan lowered himself into a chair opposite the old man. "Sir, you should know—"

"Should know what? That she was here on behalf of the Savannah Historical Society? That she asked me if I'd consider donating these flintlocks, which were stolen from a Southern plantation during the Civil War? That she knew they had no legal claim to them, but hoped I'd consider it as a good-faith gesture and an excellent tax write-off?"

Ryan sagged back into the chair, completely stunned. He could hardly take it in. Jade had come here in complete honesty? She'd asked the man to donate an antique, probably worth upward of fifty-thousand dollars, and he'd *agreed*?

Though, heaven knew, when Jade Maguire set her mind to have something, any man was hopeless to resist. Including this old guy.

"Do you mean to tell me she didn't come here saying she was some kind of buyer? Or gun expert? Or appraiser?" he asked, feeling two steps behind everyone else in the world.

"Course not," the old man snapped, rapping his cane on the wood floor. "Can't imagine why you'd think otherwise, but she contacted me weeks ago, telling me who she was and who she represented." Then he raised a sly brow. "But you didn't know that, did you? You thought she was here for some other reason altogether."

Yeah. To steal something that had once been stolen.

Ryan could only nod.

"And you've been lying to her all along about things? I heard that much." Then he cackled. "Naked and tied to a statue, eh? I'd like to know who this Mamie Brandywine is."

Ryan shuddered. "No, you wouldn't."

"That young lady, she got you good, didn't she?" He cackled again, then let out another sound, something like a harrumph. "But she didn't do it unscathed. Got herself hurt in the process."

Ryan, realizing all the implications of what the old man was saying, launched up out of the chair and began to stalk the room. "I can't understand this. She steals from my grandmother, but politely asks for something from you?"

He was speaking more to himself, so he wasn't quite prepared for Mr. Brewer to answer. "Your grandmother?"

Ryan nodded absently. "She called me for help, saying Jade had swindled her out of a painting."

"You a married man?"

The abrupt subject change didn't seem any more crazy than anything else that had happened in the past few minutes. Ryan shook his head. "No."

"In love with Miss Maguire?"

He merely nodded.

"Grandmother a matchmaking type?"

Then he froze and turned on his heel. Gape-jawed, he stared at the old man.

Mr. Brewer started to laugh. "Worried for a long time about my youngest boy getting hooked up with the wrong one. Tried everything to steer him toward a young woman who used to work for me, but he wouldn't have it." He nodded his head in obvious satisfaction. "'Til I locked 'em together in a storage closet at a Christmas party one year."

And suddenly, Ryan got it.

He closed his eyes, shaking his head, wondering when his brain had turned into a complete wasteland.

Suckered. He'd been completely suckered. Played like a kindergartner tricked into giving up his lunch money.

By his own grandmother.

13

JADE HAD STOPPED CRYING by the time she got home to her apartment in Savannah that night. She'd cried a lot while racing to the airport, not even caring about the things she'd left behind at Ryan's place. She'd tried to hide the tears behind dark glasses but probably hadn't fooled anyone on the flight home to Georgia.

And on the drive from the airport, she'd just given in and whined, right up until she'd entered her apartment.

"Damn him," she muttered late that night as she tore off her clothes and reached for a comfortable, familiar nightshirt in her top dresser drawer.

She couldn't believe how...how *raw* she felt, still, all these hours later. But those moments in Mr. Brewer's apartment—those few dangerous moments when she'd asked him to believe in her and he'd responded with silence—seemed like they were going to repeat in her brain for the rest of her life.

A thief, of all things.

She was used to the women in her family being called names. A witch, a terror, they'd called Lula Mae. A man-eater, her mother had been named. A tease, a bimbo they'd said about Jenny. As for her? Jade? The one who'd considered herself the reasonable, responsible, driven, hardworking one?

She'd heard seductress. She'd heard brazen. She'd even heard dangerous.

But, by God, she'd never heard thief. Not until the man she loved had called her that.

"Damn you, Ryan," she muttered as she curled up in her bed, hugging her pillow. She wished Jinx was around. He was a cat, therefore often aloof. He did, however, seem to know when Jade needed comfort. He gave her the sweetest kitty kisses when he knew she needed them the most. Right now, she wanted to cling to him like a drowning woman held a life preserver.

She couldn't pick up Jinx from Tally's, however, without picking up Lula Mae. Jade wasn't up to that. Commiserating with Lula Mae meant downing gallons of oddly spiced tea, hearing the old woman's riddles about love, and plotting payback.

"Maybe later."

For now she had to grieve, alone, over what she'd lost—something that she'd only this morning begun to believe she'd found. True love.

"Ha!" she snorted, thrusting the very idea of it away.

Sleep proving elusive, Jade lay in bed for a long time, still trying to put everything together. She knew the basics. Ryan had come to Savannah to seek her out, *after* he'd sought out her little sister up in New York.

He'd thought she'd stolen something and wanted… what? Recompense? Retribution? Revenge? All of the above?

She remembered that first night, all his intuitive questions, when she'd half-jokingly asked if he was a P.I. instead of an architect. If she hadn't just been in his home, seen the drawings and blueprints all over his home office, she'd suspect that he really was a private investigator. But she knew he wasn't.

No, he hadn't been hired to track her down. It had been entirely personal. She just couldn't understand why.

Finally, sheer exhaustion made her give in to a turbulent night's sleep full of disturbing dreams.

She still hadn't figured things out the next day. Ryan tried to call—she heard his voice on the answering machine, but she refused to pick up. His messages said he'd made a mistake, that he hadn't understood, had been misled. That he had to talk to her, to set things right.

But how could he set something like that right? How could they go back to the beginning and pretend he hadn't been lying to her and he hadn't believed her to be a completely different person than she was? How could she ever really believe he was honest when he said he needed her in his life, that he cared about her, when he obviously didn't know her at all?

Because she didn't want to see anyone and have to explain her tear-stained face, she didn't tell anyone she was back in town. Somehow, however, Daisy suspected. The young woman called late that afternoon, her voice sounding frenzied on Jade's answering machine. "Look, I know you're out of town, but if you pick up this message, please call me. Freddy called in sick, and we have this big private tour tonight, a special one leaving out of your uncle's place. And I have the regular group to take out. Help!"

Jade bit back a curse, vowing to fire Freddy first thing tomorrow even though the new people she'd hired weren't fully up to speed yet. Then she grabbed the phone. "I'm here, Daisy."

"Oh, thank you! I didn't know what to do."

"Freddy's now unemployed. I'm the camel and this is the last straw."

"About time," the young woman muttered.

"Now, what's this about a private tour?" They did private group tours on occasion, but Jade didn't remember scheduling any for this week. In fact, she'd felt comfortable going away for a few days precisely because she'd had the two new people, plus Daisy and Freddy, and no extra tours on the schedule.

"Sorry, it just came in. A group going out of the Winter Garden, because they're staying there or something. Tonight at nine. Freddy was supposed to take it, since I have the regular late-night tour. But he's a no-show. And those two new ones don't know the haunted stuff yet. They've just barely gotten the history for the day tours!"

Jade muttered a low curse, then sighed heavily. There was no escaping it. This was part of running her own business. "Don't worry about it, Daisy—I'll take the tour. Let the clients know I'll meet them in the parlor of the Winter Garden at nine sharp."

That's how Jade ended up knocking on the door to her Uncle Henry's place at 8:55 p.m. It was dark out, a steamy night full of the calls of cicadas and the scents of the South—wet earth, thick sweet perfumes of the night-blooming jasmine Henry grew around the place, and that spicy, late-night aroma of mystery that Savannah wore around itself like some women wore a heady perfume.

She hardly noticed as she pushed a pair of dark-tinted sunglasses over her puffy red eyes. Hopefully the tour group would think she was merely eccentric and mysterious. Not teary-eyed and heartbroken.

She only hoped she didn't break anything else by tripping over something in the dark.

"Right this way, Miss Maguire," Henry's maid said when she opened the door.

Mutely following the woman to the parlor, Jade stepped inside. Instead of coming in with her, the maid closed the door, leaving Jade alone. "Wait," she said, realizing no one else was in the room, "there's nobody..."

That's when she noticed the flowers. They were everywhere, filling antique vases and delicately cut crystal bowls. They rested on every surface in the room—each table, the mantelpiece, the baby grand piano.

Magnolias. Profusions of the giant flowers, white and moist as if they'd just been cut. And with them, great clumps of orange blossoms. The effect was intoxicating. A mix of sweet, heady perfume and citrus and...

"Coconut oil?"

She yanked her sunglasses off her face, scanning every corner of the room.

"Hello, Jade."

Ryan.

He rose from a chair in the corner, where he'd been sitting quietly since she'd entered.

She whirled around and reached for the doorknob. It wouldn't twist. "Uncle Henry," she said with a groan.

"I asked him to give us five minutes," Ryan said softly as he crossed the room. "Five minutes for me to try to convince you that even though I'm the biggest loser in the world, you should give me a second chance."

She clenched her jaw, then her fists, trying to gain control over her wildly swinging emotions. Jade wasn't ready to deal with this. Not now. Not here. Not while surrounded with these heady smells that reminded her of him. Of them.

The magnolias in the garden that very first wild

night. The citrus and coconut from their day at the beach. He'd had her heart clenching with the memories before her brain had the opportunity to force them away.

"You fight dirty," she whispered, still not turning around to face him.

He touched her shoulder, gently, not demanding, but silently pleading with her to look at him. When the tips of his fingers caressed the side of her neck, she let out a little moan, but remained frozen, staring at the dark wood paneling of the door.

"Let me talk to you, Jade."

"Go ahead," she said, fighting to remain stiff and unyielding. "Try to explain why I should believe a word a liar like you would say."

She could feel his entire body flinch—he was that close. But he didn't back off. "You're right. I'm a liar and an untrusting bastard. I came to Savannah to find you and get back a painting I thought you'd stolen from my grandmother."

She jerked her head to look at him over her shoulder. "What painting?"

He met her stare evenly. "The LeBeuf portrait hanging at the Martinique house."

The painting she'd acquired last month. The one she'd *legally* acquired last month.

"She told me you'd stolen it."

"Who?"

"The woman who gave it to you." He shook his head in disgust. "My grandmother."

That shocked her into finally turning around. But she stayed close to the door, backing against it to keep some physical distance between them. Thankfully Ryan didn't move forward or try to crowd her.

"Those nice people, the Graysons, are your grand-parents?"

He nodded.

"Why would she tell you the painting was stolen?"

"I'm not sure you'll believe this."

She crossed her arms. "Try me. I happen to be slightly more trusting than some people."

His eyes flared. She'd scored a hit. She wondered why that didn't give her even a moment of satisfaction.

"She wanted me to meet you."

Of all the things she'd expected to hear, that was no-where near the top five. Ryan's grandmother had re-ported her valuable painting stolen because she wanted her grandson to *meet* the woman who'd sup-posedly stolen it?

He must have seen her look of derision. "You don't understand my family. I come from a long line of pas-sionately romantic people."

Passionate. Oh, she could concede that. In spite of his cool, cultured, big-city facade, Ryan had exhibited depths of passion she'd never before seen in a man, as well as a daring spirit that had totally captivated her from that very first night. "Okay, I can believe that."

He looked relieved. "Unfortunately, I've never really accepted that about myself. My relationships have been okay. Nothing that knocked me off my feet. No one who ever inspired me to think I could fall madly in love, like my parents, grandparents and sister did. That happened to drive my rather controlling grandmother a little crazy."

She'd liked his grandmother quite a lot, but she could see the potential for controlling. The woman had asked Jade a ton of personal questions during their af-ternoon together. Including questions about Jade's love life. And marital status.

"I can't believe it," she whispered, bringing her hands to her lips as the truth dawned. "She was *match-making?*"

Ryan nodded, giving a helpless shrug. "She knew I'd never let her set me up. She's tried that too many times." He finally stepped closer, touching her arm— a featherlight touch that told her he was being honest but didn't intimidate. "She also knew you were perfect for me. That you were the soul mate I'd never really believed I had. That I'd fall madly in love with you and be unable to imagine my life without you in it."

Her heart thudded in her chest. Those green eyes of his, those beautiful eyes that darkened when Ryan was aroused, or sparkled when he was amused, shone clear and bright with the truth of his emotions.

"I love you, Jade. My grandmother's lie got me down here. But you…once I met you…I never wanted to leave." He raised his hand to cup her cheek, delicately stroking his fingertips over her cheekbone, wiping away a bit of moisture Jade hadn't even known had dripped out of her eye. "I'm sorry for what my family did to you. But I'm not sorry I came." His voice lowered, nearly shaking with intensity as he repeated, "I *love* you."

Her heart quivered again and her pulse sped up. Oh, she wanted to believe him. Wanted more than anything to believe him. His words were beautiful, his expression sincere, his touch divine. But it didn't erase everything that had happened.

"If you love me, how could you believe I'd…I'd be a thief?" Her voice broke a little, and she still kept her body stiff and straight, separated from his by mere inches as she demanded an answer to the most important question of all.

"I didn't, not really," he admitted.

"You did a good impersonation of it yesterday morning in Mr. Brewer's apartment."

He clarified. "I mean, at first, when my grandmother told me you'd stolen from her, I had no choice but to believe. As I got to know you, I realized I wasn't seeing the whole picture. Then when we visited the Martinique house, and I saw the painting, I began to understand."

She didn't quite follow, but she listened as Ryan continued, his fingers still gently caressing her face.

"I know you have a strong conscience, Jade. You have a strong sense of right and wrong, a strong loyalty to this place, its history and its culture. So it suddenly made sense to me, you see, that you'd want to return important artifacts to their rightful places. Like someone might want to return a statue from a looted tomb back to its pyramid in Egypt. You'd never steal for personal gain, only to right an old injustice."

She saw the honesty in his eyes, the tender smile he didn't try to hide.

"We were together both before and after we visited the Martinique house," she whispered, beginning to believe, to open up and take in the warmth radiating off the man.

He nodded. "Yes, we were. I was falling in love with you. Both before and after. But after, I began to understand you. To admire you for doing what you thought was right, even as I was terrified that you'd get hurt or get caught. I was determined to protect you."

The weight that she'd felt on her shoulders for the past thirty-six hours suddenly seemed to lift. Ryan might have thought she'd stolen something. His own grandmother, who he obviously loved, had flat-out *said* she had. But once he'd gotten to know her he'd never thought she was a common low *thief*. Even more, he hadn't judged her for it. Hadn't condemned her.

In fact, he'd loved her.

She took a deep breath, closing her eyes and trying to analyze her feelings. That breath filled her mind with the scents he'd surrounded her with. All the memories they'd created in the short weeks they'd known each other, the scent memories that would live inside her until the day she died. The ones that would remind her for the rest of her life that she loved this man, and *only* this man.

Her anger seeped away, replaced not only by understanding and forgiveness, but also heart-clenching love. She lifted a trembling hand and covered his hand on her face, then pulled it to her mouth to press a kiss on his palm.

"Oh, Jade," he whispered as he drew her close. "Can you forgive me?" He kissed her temple, rubbing his cheek against hers. "Can we call my doubt of you a mix of summer insanity and flower intoxication?"

She laughed softly.

"Not to mention," he added, "too much of your aunt Lula Mae's tea and a man who didn't believe in madness-inspiring love trying to find any reason to escape from his own destiny?"

Destiny. Sounded reasonable. Especially here in this rich, sultry place on this wicked, hot summer night.

"You're forgiven," she said, drawing his mouth close to hers for a long, lingering kiss. There was instant fire, as always, but also the slow, languorous, bone-melting emotion that had been present between them from the first night they'd made love—right in this very house.

"I think I can even forgive your grandmother," she added as they drew apart.

"I paid her back," Ryan said with a lift of his brow. "Right now she's so terrified her lies have cost me you forever that she hasn't even realized how successful her plan actually was."

Jade laughed softly, picturing the meddlesome woman in just such a state. "Let's not tell her for a while."

He joined her laughter. "You're a wicked woman."

"You wouldn't have me any other way."

"No, I wouldn't."

She curled her fingers into his hair to hold him close, meeting his stare so she could gift him with the same kind of declaration he'd given her. She'd never said the words to a man because she'd never felt them for anyone but Ryan.

The time had come. She was a Maguire. She loved hard. She'd love only once. She loved *him.*

"I love you, Ryan. I'll love you forever."

He showed her his pleasure by kissing her, tasting her, inhaling her as he held her tightly against his body as if he'd never let her go.

Maybe he wouldn't.

Which was just fine with Jade.

Epilogue

LYNNETTE GRAYSON SPOTTED the small jewelry box in her husband's shaving kit as they finished unpacking at the Winter Garden, where they were staying for Thanksgiving weekend. Edward was already anticipating Aunt Lula Mae's famous cornbread stuffing, so he wasn't paying attention as his wife began to dig through his things. "What's this?" she asked.

"That's nothing," he said with a harrumph as he tried to snatch the small velvet box from her hand.

She smiled, knowing at once what it meant. When she finally got him to open it and saw the lovely old wedding ring that her late mother-in-law had worn, she sighed in pleasure.

"Keep your nose out of it," Edward said, shaking his finger at her. "Let the boy propose in his own way. Ryan's just barely forgiven you for your shenanigans. And if you get yourself uninvited for Thanksgiving dinner tomorrow at Jade's mama's house, I'll...I'll go without you!"

He didn't mean it, of course. The sparkle in Edward's fine blue eyes told her he was just as happy as she that her scheme to bring Ryan together with the perfect woman had worked.

She wasn't one to brag...but she'd really *done* it.

She'd found the right woman for her boy. Ryan was madly in love with Jade Maguire, and she loved him right back. Anyone with eyes could see that.

The only problem was this whole moving to Savannah business. She hadn't anticipated that. Since when did the man move for the woman? Such things simply weren't done in her day.

But that's what had happened. Ryan had quit his job, packed his belongings, loaded that great slobbery dog of his in his car and driven south mere weeks after he'd first heard Jade Maguire's name. At least he'd found a job quickly, thanks to his work on the article about Savannah's architecture.

Ah, well, she supposed there were worse things than a grandson who lived several states away and served things like collard greens at Thanksgiving dinner.

Like a grandson who never found his soul mate, never fell madly in love, never truly glowed with happiness.

That would be worse. Much worse.

No worry of that anymore. Not for Ryan. Not for any member of her family. Which was exactly the way Lynnette Grayson planned to keep it.

"Are you ready?" her husband asked as he draped a wrap over her shoulders, giving her a slight squeeze that told her she was forgiven for being so meddlesome. How could he not forgive her, since she'd never known any other way to be?

"More than ready," she said, already bouncing on her toes with excitement about tonight's adventure.

Ghosts and murder. Vengeance and love affairs. Scandal and mystery. Yes, she was fully prepared to enjoy an evening with her future granddaughter-in-law, hearing Jade do what she did best—introduce Savannah. And make all who visited fall under her spell.

Just like Ryan had.

eHARLEQUIN.com
The Ultimate Destination for Women's Fiction

Visit eHarlequin.com's Bookstore today
for today's most popular books at great prices.

- An extensive selection of romance books by top authors!

- Choose our convenient "bill me" option. No credit card required.

- New releases, Themed Collections and hard-to-find backlist.

- A sneak peek at upcoming books.

- Check out book excerpts, book summaries and Reader Recommendations from other members and post your own too.

- Find out what everybody's reading in Bestsellers.

- Save BIG with everyday discounts and exclusive online offers!

- Our Category Legend will help you select reading that's exactly right for you!

- Visit our Bargain Outlet often for huge savings and special offers!

- Sweepstakes offers. Enter for your chance to win special prizes, autographed books and more.

**Your purchases are 100%
guaranteed—so shop online
at www.eHarlequin.com today!**

The world's bestselling romance series.

Seduction and Passion Guaranteed!

THE PRINCESS BRIDES

For duty, for money…for passion!

Discover a thrilling new trilogy from a rising star of Harlequin Presents®, Jane Porter!

Meet the Royals…

Chantal, Nicolette and Joelle are members of the blue-blooded Ducasse family. Step inside their sophisticated and glamorous world and watch as these beautiful princesses find they have to marry three international playboys—for duty, for money… and definitely for passion!

Don't miss

THE SULTAN'S BOUGHT BRIDE (#2418)
September 2004

THE GREEK'S ROYAL MISTRESS (#2424)
October 2004

THE ITALIAN'S VIRGIN PRINCESS (#2430)
November 2004

Pick up a Harlequin Presents® novel and you will enter a world of spine-tingling passion and provocative, tantalizing romance!

Available wherever Harlequin books are sold.

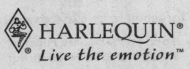

HARLEQUIN®
Live the emotion™